THE TO-LET HOUSE

Daisy Hasan

TARA BOOKS

This is a work of fiction. Any similarity or resemblance to any events or persons living or dead is purely coincidental.

The To-Let House

First published in English by Tara Books
and Tara Publishing Ltd., UK

Copyright © 2010 Daisy Hasan

Cover Design: Avinash Veeraraghavan

Tara Books, Chennai, India <www.tarabooks.com>

Printed and bound by The Indcom press, Chennai - 600 042.

ISBN: 978-81-906756-5-9

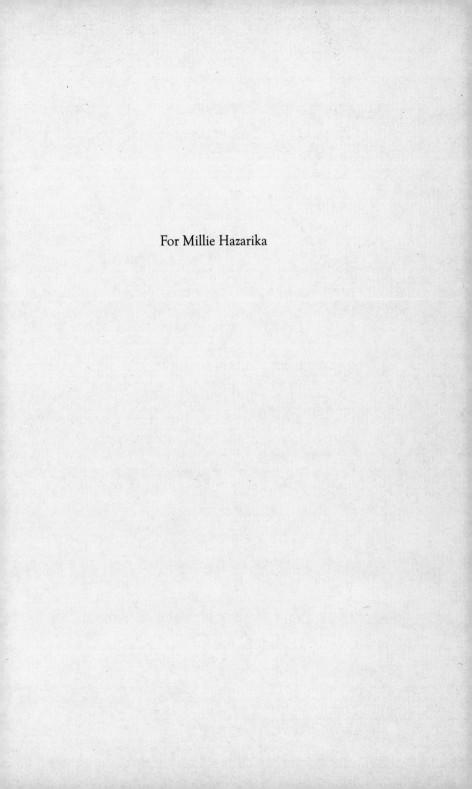

For Millie Hazarika

Shillong cracks open like a child's storybook. Its pages are stuck together from being closed so long. It is raining on the first page. The water runs through all the big colour pictures, which are turning white with rage at the rowdy rain.

In my memory it is such and we are still young.

Clemmie, her brother Kulay, my sister Addy and I, Di.

We are always young, always in love, always splintering into pieces as we come towards each other.

We are children just within reach of happiness but always falling short. We are incoherent with magic and meanness and sting each other out of sheer concern.

Our mothers and fathers torment us and we love them. Our mothers and fathers are tormented and they love us. If they go away we learn to wait for them until the day they never come. If we go away they wait for us as if they are not waiting.

In my memory I see them all. All the mothers and the fathers, all the sisters and the brothers, all the friends and the lovers lying in wait for each other.

THE MANSION
(1979)

1. THE FAMILY IN THE MANSION

Kulay, a fair, skinny, whip-wielding boy with grey, stony eyes, guards the border between a Shillong mansion, once home to a British tea planter, and its drab tenants' quarters. A forget-me-not hedge separates the drab houses from the magnificent mansion.

He is twelve and is wearing a red polo-neck sweater. He dances in circles like a ribbon of stony sunlight.

May, his mother, is standing at the brass-knobbed door of the mansion, her head barely visible to Kulay over the ancient black Aston Martin (A90 Atlantic) parked in the porch. Ignoring the scrubbing sounds that Redcoat, her maid, makes as she polishes the wooden floors indoors, May gazes across her well mown lawn into the distance. Neat beds of sweet peas line the gravelled walk up to the imperial mansion that stands sulking beneath its haughty red roof. Its lace-curtained windows, like so many eyes staring out of its creamy walls, grow hazy under the smoke creeping up from the stylishly angled chimney.

'Aieee Kulay...' May screams at the white monkey in the red polo-neck who has climbed the highest branches of the plum tree and is hanging by his feet, trying to watch the world go by—upside-down.

He sees an upside-down Seventh Day Adventist church, separated from the fire brigade building by a balding field. An unhurried road borders his upturned vision of the world. A road on which a few cream-blue buses with a dash of red on the side, dash to and fro between the taxis. The taxis play up Elvis against Cliff, Cliff against Elvis, ducking the 'sha-lew, sha-lew' calls of market-headed buses. An upside-down procession, shouting slogans, passes by. To the right of the Meghalaya Fire Service building is a fatigued mosque, grown white in the face by the diurnal cries of a wispy muezzin.

The upside-down boy notes with disdain that the dome of the mosque is not as big as another he has seen—the dome of the gurudwara further away which, for him, qualifies as 'The World's Biggest Momo.'

His sullen mouth breaks into a sudden smile. He is neither a Momodome nor a Mohammedan, but a blue-blooded, stone-eyed Khasi. He knows he is different—cleaner and clearer than them, the outsiders.

To keep from getting distracted by May's 'Aieee Kulaaaay...' nuisance, he tries to discern the limits of his sight. He looks past the green and red-roofed houses hidden among the hilltop pines, past the furthest range of mountains said to be hanging by their hair to the high Himalayas. His thoughts grow fuzzy and turn to the kites in the sky. He watches a kite go up, up, up until he falls down, down, down with the kite into the sky.

May continues to call for him though her cries become softer as her thoughts turn to how closely her mansion resembles an English manor. How opportune, she thinks, that my father, Hilarious L, bagged this house when he did.

The late Hilarious L had been a well-connected, highflying man. May recalls how he had once justified this highflying lifestyle in an interview to a reporter who was profiling the corrupt bureaucrats of the state.

'You see...' began Hilarious L, angling his ass to get out his handkerchief from the pocket of his stiffly ironed grey trousers, 'You see... I am talking... I am serious...'

There was a long pause during which May, then a young girl of sixteen, had entered with two glasses of brightly bouncing orange juice. She had surreptitiously taken a sip out of both glasses hoping to infect the interviewer and interviewee with her tonsillitis condition.

'Presume, for example, that I am corrupt. I take bribes... I use my official position for non-official purposes. I do this because why?'

The questioner had no answers.

Hilarious L paused to sip from his glass and grimacing at the sour bacterial concoction, resumed with raised voice, 'I maust have servants. I maust attend parties and other social fonkshons... both official and non-official. When I go out for marketing or on a social courtesy visit, I should not walk.'

The interviewer seemed unconvinced.

'Or even if I do,' persisted Hilarious L, his blood pressure rising, 'My wife maust not! Because why,' he barked.

There was no response.

'Because,' he continued, 'Because an offisore's wife is a MAHARRRRANI!

My wife must be well-dressed when she goes out, otherwise salesmen at the counter will address her as 'Didi' instead of 'Maadom' and her host will not see her off at the roadside. Besides I have social obligations and the responsibility to educate my children...'

'Yes sir...,' squeaked the interviewer, for he had kept quiet long enough and his throat needed some clearing.

Standing at the door of the magnificent house, this ludicrous scene from the past fades from her vacant eyes and May's thoughts return to the present. They drift towards the To-Let House in the backwaters of the mansion where she has ousted an ill-mannered Assamese tenant and his extra-tall white wife for he wouldn't accept a hike in the rent.

The two-room-one-bathroom To-Let House stands apologetically under its unpainted roof, though the spindly orange trees at its front do their best to lend it some colour. It has no stylishly or otherwise angled chimney. A straightforward 'To-Let' sign stands at its front like a 'Kick Me' note stuck by a school bully on an unsuspecting back. A dull, rusty tin gate separates it from the lane that runs along the back of the mansion.

May disappears into the house but reappears when the doorbell rings. Redcoat stops her polishing. She makes towards the door in response to the doorbell's elegant ding-dong. She is overtaken by May who gives her a cold stare.

Opening the door herself, May sees a family of three women, two wee and one wise, walking up to the mansion in their small and skinny state, visibly shaken by the tribulations they have had to endure to get so far.

The mother of the girls carries a hanger from which hangs – incongruity of incongruities – a peach-coloured wedding sari with an apology of gold brocade and a splash of blue along the border. They are led by Borthakur, the firefighter who occupies one of May's many tenant quarters. He has rung the doorbell and is asking the straggly procession, marching beneath the invisible banner of hope, to hurry up.

The two girls fall in line, taking in the prospect of the field and 'the faraway', as ten-year-old Addy calls it, for the sights are too much for the mites to make sense of. Perhaps, they think, this is the start of something new, though the clammy hand of their Ma seems to suggest that this is the end. Still, she tries to appear calm.

Nine-year-old me notices a red upside-down blob amidst the lush branches of a faraway tree. At first I think it's a biggish sort of plum but the plum has a bum – which has turned numb – and is beginning to descend. A plump, tablecloth-clad question mark peers cautiously from behind the door. The Numb Bum keeps a safe distance. Ma stands face-to-face with May, feeling like an uprooted, parched plant waiting to be watered.

'I haf no mony,' announces May's red mouth in a face that is gleaming with greed and gumption. A flattened pancake of a face that is still secretly beautiful. May's eyes glint when they catch the setting sun. She is grounded by the weight of her gold jewellery but hoists herself up on her high heels and squints down at Ma, ignoring Borthakur who is making weak introductions.

'Aieeeeee Governaar!' May shouts, suddenly energised by an idea.

'Oi?'

A tall, dark head looms up behind May while a freckled nine-year-old fountain called Clemmie gushes out from between them and races towards Numb Bum Kulay.

Governor is wearing patched pantaloons and brown canvas shoes. He has not and will not graduate from local liquor to IMFL – Indian Made Foreign Liquor – for he is not an ass licker, he tells Ma, who is on the verge of collapse.

'I'm a Khasi,' he announces proudly trying to shove May (who will not be shoved and sticks to her Christian ground). 'She's a Christian but we live in harmonies. Seng and Song live in harmonies,' he chuckles, 'but she has no monies... Hilarious. Hilarious Father-in-law!'

We look up and they look down.

Governor frowns at May.

'She's a Kong,' he roars. 'But I am a King... I'm the King of the Kong, the Seng of the Song... ha ha! Hear me sing.'

We strain our eager ears to hear the story of the ousted Assamese tenant – 'A-Siamese man' as Governor calls him – who had silver streaks in his hair. Who wore pink shirts and yellow ties and beat the shit out of his taller-than-him wife.

'She was from Fishland,' Governor says, grimacing at his failing memory. 'FINLAND,' squeaks a voice beneath a shock of wild hair. Ma pinches my palm instead of Addy's, who has dared to speak.

'Ohhh Fishland... ney... Finland... I forgot,' says Governor. 'BUT—he beat the shit out of her. Ha! Ha!'

The three versions of each other – big, small and skinny-small – shiver weakly. Meanwhile, May is sizing up the curious trio that stands in the porch, much to the astonishment of Clemmie and Kulay, who keep a safe distance but listen intently. May notes that the woman is neither A-Siamese, nor A-Bengali, though she wears a sari.

A malleable tenant, she thinks. Fit to inhabit the To-Let House should she ask for it. This woman who is seen but not heard.

Before Ma knows it the deed is done. A woman without a husband is, in May's opinion, the thing to be. She informs Ma of a secretarial vacancy at the Conservation Centre, sticking out her hand for an advance on the rent.

'Beat the shit out of her,' Governor continues, 'because why? Because I saw her washing her pants!'

> Yellow yellow
> Dirty fellow

Addy flinches as her suspicions are confirmed. She tucks her abundant hair behind her ears and insists that 'To-Let' is 'Toilet' with a forgotten 'I.' The trio walk weakly towards the To-Let House.

Once inside, Ma fiercely locks the door against the world and sets about making herself scarce. The world, her expression tells Addy and me, is a bubble waiting to burst. It is a big red balloon that has slid through a child's fingers and is wafting up into the air achingly out of reach. And love – that huge, gigantic love that had swelled her belly twice – has turned into a brittle twig that snaps every time you step on it.

I move towards an ancient wooden cupboard. Perhaps my father is standing inside. But the cupboard stares back at me like a coffin without a corpse.

Ma flings open the cupboard doors wider. She presses her thin lips together, burying the wedding sari inside. It will hang in the sparse cupboard, untouched for years like Ma herself hung around, untouched and dust-laden.

'If they ask you about your father just say he's posted outside somewhere...'

In our mind's eye Addy and I see a bearded man inside an envelope, but we know better than to speak.

Ma hitches up her sari and picks up the spade lying in a corner of the room. She digs up the earth around the thorny lemon and spindly orange trees and buries her past along with the seeds for the peas and the beans that will inaugurate her kitchen garden.

When the peas and the beans grow, we tug at them, but though we pull at the creepers, we can never entirely pull her past out.

2. TAKING SOIL

Perhaps he will come and see me, thinks Ma, as she unties a bundle of hurriedly packed clothes, which fall clumsily onto the floor in the To-Let House. Her heart winces at the thought of him, her one-time husband.

'Husband,' she says aloud to herself and laughs a little. The word sounds mirthful and bitter. He never actually married her, but marriage was what it had been about. His marriage to someone else. His unmarrying someone else to marry her. His choosing to marry someone else instead of her. Then, to top it all, his insistence on reversing roles and becoming her wife.

She moves towards the cupboard, resolving to get a grip on herself and hang up the crumpled clothes. Yet when she opens the creaking wooden door, a younger version of her man steps out through the jangling hangers and rising dust, putting her memory back on its loop again.

'How long have I been away from this place that I love?' he says in Ma's reverie, just as he had done bursting into her secluded life in Shillong at the age of twenty nine.

It was true that the last time she had seen him he had been in green 'half-pants'—an oleaginous child of twelve with his finger in his nose. She was scarcely ten.

They had stood together at a school friend's birthday party not knowing what to do. She knew her dress wasn't right. He had already been humiliated by the assembled guests, for added to the fact that he was not a Khasi but an outsider – a *dkhar* – he'd had the temerity to turn up in less than full trousers.

His eyes darted around furtively as he tried to shake off the gaze that had fixed itself on his hairy limbs. He produced a box of matches from the pockets of his derided trousers and commanded her to hold the matchsticks upright.

'Hold them tight,' he said tensely.

'Look,' he addressed his audience nervously. 'Watch the trick.' He ran the matchbox expertly over the matchsticks in her hands. Her fingers singed but she pretended she had been in the know. The party laughed and clapped heartily as the lights cast a little glow over his cloudy face.

Her lips trembled when she blew out the matchsticks.

'It's called being an opportunist...' he said, conscious that he had used a big English word, which might endear him further to the rich Khasi boys and girls. And it had. She was now the poor duped *dkhar* girl. And she stood in the centre of the room in her flared pants and her too-long shirt as the children went around her shouting: 'Lina, stupid Dumbelina, now she's the Queen of the idiot's court.'

The children's chant buzzes in Ma's head as she stands in the To-Let House, many years removed from that unhappy childhood day. She soon realises that this is no chant of yore but sounds from the human train that Addy and Di have turned into to amuse themselves. She moves towards them determined to put an end to their merriment when a man, undeniably her man, steps in again, considerably grown since his earlier entry.

His hair, always unruly, now reached his shoulders and an ill-advised beard lent an air of depth to everything he said. And he had a lot to say.

'How long have I been away from this place that I love?' he said, arrogantly sitting himself down on her bed in her parents' home. He had returned from a world beyond this very small world she knew. 'And in that world,' he said, 'Shillong was just a dot of desire.'

She laughed through her bad teeth. They sat talking late into the night. Stories wafted out with his sultry smoke rings. She had noticed the disapproving silence that had descended on her home after he had entered but she didn't care. And they slipped away. Into the teashops where the Kongs looked at the strange man and the girl who spoke to them in Khasi asking for several cups of red tea.

'Sha-saw,' he repeated the Khasi word for milkless tea after her. He looked around the teashop, taking in its frail tin walls. A man sat on the edge of his bench listening to film songs on a transistor. Another moved his grey head from side to side and shut his eyes as he chewed on his food. A baby tied to her mother's back sucked her thumb and stared at him.

'I quite like this makeshift-ness.' He wondered if he could take a photograph.

His paunch bulged through his long grey sweater and his rough feet betrayed signs of the struggle he had endured on the long road that had led him away from home in search of a nobler life.

The prodigal son, who had left Shillong aged seventeen, had returned to his town rather disenchanted by the city he had seen. He had come to realise that though an outsider, he could only ever belong here. For it was here, and only here, that he might save himself from the anonymity he had been plunged into, the moment he crossed Shillong's borders. And anonymity he could not live with. Indifference he could not tolerate.

As if to confirm his convictions, a mad man had approached him as he stood waiting for the train that would take him away from the alien city forever.

'Go home. Put your house in order,' commanded the soothsayer. 'Go home... how long will you keep running from yourself? Put your house in order. Go home!'

Ma looked away shyly as his eyes burnt into hers. He leaned further towards her and looking straight into her eyes said, 'This chit of a girl has grown.'

Suddenly, to the vagabond, Shillong seemed to offer an enticing sojourn. 'What if I, son of a lifelong academic,' said he, rising from the wooden bench in the tea stall, 'stayed here a while? What if I imparted a bit of myself to this tiny town, for it does seem that this tiny town has need of me.'

Years of living on the edge had made him reckless. He looked at her and felt that she would love him. 'Dumbelina...'

Will you get angry if you find me at your door again?

Will you get angry if I enter your room?

Will you read to me at two in the night?

Will you wake up at four to see the moon?

Will you bail me out of jail?

Will you buy me books?

Will you eat my dinners and drink my drinks?

Will you put your head in the crook of my arm?

Will you wait for me?

Will you let your hair turn grey with mine?

Will you die if I die?

He was breathless and though he had not spoken aloud, he was sincere.

Will you mother my dust-laden children?

Will you love me always?

His dust-laden children are still playing train in the To-Let House. Addy, the storehouse of sensible sentences and sounds, hums with the turning train wheels and hugs her whimsical name: 'Addy-Addy. The girl without her Daddy.'

Ma's mouth twists with bitterness. 'You two,' she shakes her finger threateningly, hitching up her long jet black hair into a bun high up on her head and hitting Di the Dunce for having smuggled her finger into her ear again.

'I want the breeze Ma. I want the breeeeeeze.' I'm hot and cross. I can feel it in my thighs.

'You'll get it if you open the window.'

Addy climbs onto a chair and opens the window. Through the orange trees she can see slices of the street where women wearing long, checked tablecloths pinned at the shoulders are selling pineapples.

'Kong. Kong,' calls a man from across the road.

'Kong. Kong. King Kong!' echoes Addy, the wild-haired word worm with eyes as wide as wonder, laughing in her yellow T-shirt. Addy's yellow T-shirt says 'Friend or Foe' and it has a rocket, coloured green-red.

I never understand the rocket joke.

Addy says, 'Look there's a rocket.'

'Where?' I have to respond.

'In your pocket,' Addy sings back.

I never get it.

'I'm not getting the view now. I want the breeeeeezzzzeee and the vieeeeeeew.'

'She wants a world view, Ma,' says the precocious little girl. But soon Addy casts philosophy to the breeze and screams, 'See, see those people—their mouths are full of blood.'

Addy knows their mouths are actually reddened by the juice of *kwai* – the betel leaf and areca nut they are crunching – but she likes to imagine otherwise.

Later, Addy and I will turn into *kwai* fiends ourselves. But for now we want to make-believe, for we are small and skinny.

When Ma returns to her memories, he is already on his way to meet a prospective employer.

Since Ma had not been privy to this conversation, a plane passes overhead in her reverie, rendering their words inaudible to her ears.

He returned to Ma's door several times after this. Each time he arrived, a silence descended over her house. Each time he left, the silence burst into fierce protest against her association with the vagabond. She was warned of the ill that would befall her if she continued to see him. One day, sickened by it all, she slipped out with him and never went back.

Ma knows she can never go back home. I would die, she thinks. I would die if I went back to my mother's.

She looks around and sees Addy and Di crouching under the table. She tries to say something to them. A huge tear clouds her eye.

'Go,' she screams at the crouching girls. 'Go and play with Kulay and Clemmie next door. Go. Go and mix up.'

3. MIXING UP

Addy and I come out into the garden. Oranges have fallen on the ground and Addy picks up a podgy one, peels it with her thin little fingers and stuffs the whole thing into her mouth. Her face turns into a fat little 'O' and she chases me around the garden.

> *Flowers grow on the sun,*
> *But I don't care...*

'It's nonsense. Your songs are NONSENSE,' Addy goes off to skip.

I stop singing and peep through the forget-me-not hedge that separates our house from Clemmie's. I can see a big boy on a small tricycle, who is not Numb Bum Kulay. When we open the gate and go closer, he rings his bell and says,

'Welcome! My name is Borthakur.'

A bun emerges to contradict him.

Round and fat with sugar on the top...

Clemmie wears a short white dress and her face has a million freckles. She is bursting out of her blue jumper, which has a white smiley band running round it, carrying the words, 'Just 4 Fun.'

'No, he's telling lies. His name is Kay.'

Borthakur who is not Borthakur but only Kay rings his bell again. He is a tall, dark fourteen-year-old boy and his legs stick out funnily from the tricycle. 'Come for a ride, girls,' he says in a girlish voice. But when we go near him, he lifts up our skirts and squeals, 'Apologise.'

When he spies the real Borthakur going up to his quarters, he lifts Clemmie's skirt too. 'Apologise,' he screeches. 'Borthakur apologises.'

It is the second day in the To-Let House and there is nothing to do but play. Play, play with the new children, with Kay and Clemmie all day long, until Ma earns enough to send us to school again and finds one where they don't ask too many questions.

When we cross the hedge, Kulay charges out. He does not look like Clemmie though he is her brother. His tongue hangs out of his mouth and he charges at us madly.

From inside the house, May screams, 'Kulay! You white devil...'

Kay is sunning himself at the same spot where we met him yesterday near the big garage but the tricycle is not around. When he sees us he bows. 'Welcome again. As you know my name is Borthakur.'

Addy has worn her red trousers so that no one can pull up her skirt. We can hear May screaming again. I am wearing my blue checked trousers, and I piss in them for fear of the screams and of Kulay who is chewing on a piece of red, raw beef and holding a whip. Kulay whips Kay once. Thwack. Twice. Thwack, Thwack. Then he looks at us.

'He's sissy. What are you? English?'

'No,' Sissy Kay squeaks. 'They're Hindi—their mother wears a sari.'

'O! *Hindi liah...* I'm Khasi *mein...* you want to fly kites or you want to fight?'

'Fly kites,' Addy says quickly because she is getting scared.

'Fly kites, huh... want to fly kites? Clemmie! Clemmie!'

Clemmie comes out from the kitchen door facing the garage. Her hands are full of white dust.

'What are you doing Clemmie?' Sissy Kay is still rubbing the leg that Kulay has whipped.

'Making pumpkin pie with May.' Clemmie wipes her hands on her skirt busily.

'You and your pie,' Sissy Kay sings. 'You and your pie...'

'Clemmie!' Kulay is waving his whip in the air. 'You fight with this small devil. Fight—or else I'll whip you.'

Clemmie is wearing big black boots. She kicks me. 'C'mon, c'mon lets fight *mein*.' Kulay jumps around us, thwacking his whip.

Clemmie kicks me again. My pants are wet and I'm feeling hot and cross now. I chop her in her side. She begins to cry.

Her face is full of white dust as she rubs the tears with her pumpkin pie hands.

'I'm going to whip you now,' Kulay says. 'Bend down...'

Five whips down, May opens the door.

'Don't whip the new children, you white monkey! Come,' she smiles at us. 'Come and drink some milk.'

May's house smells of bread. It is dark. In the kitchen there is a fire and May blows at the fire through a pipe.

'Come. Come. Come and have milk,' Kulay tries to smile like May but his eyes are stony. 'Come, come let's be friends mein...'

May puts a loaf of bread on her lap and cuts it up. A covered pot dances on the fire. The pumpkin pie is inside it. Addy looks at it then looks away like Ma told us to do about food. May puts the knife back in a dish of raw beef. She wipes her hands on the red-checked tablecloth that she uses as her apron.

'Clemmie, put a little butter on the bread and give it to the new children.'

Clemmie picks up the knife.

Sissy Kay comes into the kitchen. 'Now, where's your pie?'

May says something in Khasi and we know it's not meant for us. Addy puts her hand in her pocket and takes out her hanky.

May gives me a hot cup of milk. 'Hold it,' she hisses. 'My hands are burning.' I spill some of it on my pants from May's tone, and even before we drink our milk, May says, 'Go home. Go home quickly. It's time for the Witch.'

Many facts emerge on that day of our trip across the hedge. Many facts and figures.

Like:

The earlier tenant in the To-Let House, the Assamese (or A-Siamese) man was called Kiyahoi and masqueraded under this name as a respectable beater of wives. That Kiyahoi had left a trunk full of books in the To-Let House and pray, had the new *dkhar* tenants found it?

That we are to be called *dkhars*, outsiders, which means anyone from Momodomes to Mohammedans and all the other skinny-skins who come in between.

At this point, Addy intervenes to inform Kulay that in Hindi *dkhar* sounded like a burp, and would we be relegated to mere foul air? At which the white monkey informs the wise monk that his decision is final. That we are indeed *dkhars* and would have to burp our way about the world forever.

'Understood Fizzy Burp?' asks the blue-blooded brute and when, in her reluctance, Addy replies, 'Stood,' she is informed that it is a bad word in Khasi and don't you ever repeat it again.

'Stood!'

Then Sissy Kay, interpreter of the world of adults and adulteries, by virtue of the superior education he receives at Bernard's informs us that it means prostitute, and there is in the church a pious lady of that very name, though her piety has encouraged everyone to call the good woman Kong Pro.

Pro and Kong. What could the pros and cons for Pro and Kong be, Addy wonders that night in bed when my hic-hic-hiccups keep her from falling asleep.

We ponder in the dark on the facts and figures that have been pointed out to us that day. It is a dark windy night and the busy bamboos go swish-swish this way and that. We huddle close together under the dim light, impatient for the next day when Sissy Kay will unravel for us again the world of adults and adulteries.

After several consultations across the forget-me-not hedge Ma and May decide that the best school for Addy, Clemmie and me is Little Rose Convent, which lies midway between the two schools where Kulay and Kay go. We cannot contradict Ma and May. They decide what is good for us and what is not. They make up the world. They trim it and chop it and make it fit.

'You have to be worldly-wise from now on,' Ma says, thrusting a roll of brown paper at Addy, which she will need to cover her school books.

Addy clutches the roll of brown paper but only manages to look wordy-wise.

She has discovered the trunk that Kiyahoi the Horrible has left behind. It is a steel-grey seatrunk with broken brass clasps. Ma has covered the trunk with a white shroud but Addy surreptitiously lifts up its lid and crawls inside. She sits amidst the words trying to look worldly-wise as Ma has instructed her.

Words, meanwhile, fly into her head and some fly over her head. She sits herself down inside the secure sea-trunk, drunk on the dreams that she finds at the bottom of the dark blue sea.

> My *father went to sea, sea, sea,*
> *To see what he could see, see, see,*
> *But all that he could see, see, see,*
> *Was the bottom of the dark blue sea, sea, sea.*

Addy the one-eyed pirate collects, from inside the seatrunk, concise little collectibles that can, she believes, be used for crucial childhood comprehension.

Clemmie and I are together in school. At home we sit on her swing. The swing swings from the strongest branch of the plum tree.

'Addy knows how to skip. You know?'

'Yes,' Clemmie says. 'Yes, I know.'

'Skip now.'

'Why should I?'

A big girl comes out of the front door opposite the swing. She has long silky hair and smiles like a fairy. Her mouth is red from *kwai* and she is wearing dark blue jeans.

'Mujupeas!' she calls out to Clemmie.

'Yes, Gujupeas,' Clemmie replies.

'I'm going to watch a movie,' she whispers.

'With boys?' Clemmie asks.

'Sshh... Don't tell May.'

The boys come in a jeep and she says, 'Oh! They asked me to bring a shawl.' When Clemmie fetches a shawl, the big girl says, 'Mujupeas...,'

'Yes, Gujupeas,' Clemmie replies with downcast eyes.

'Don't tell lies.' She gets inside the jeep.

'Yes, Gujupeas,' Clemmie answers in a small voice.

'Who is that big girl?'

'Phoebe.'

'Phoebe? She's your sister?'

'No. My first cousin.'

'What's that?'

'Phoebe's mother and May were sisters.'

'Who is Phoebe's mother?'

'She's dead. I wish May was dead. You know she drinks. She should be dead.'

'Drinks what?'

'Whisky... drinks with Governor.'

'Who's Governor?'

'He's my father.'

'Then Sissy Kay is he your second cousin?'

'No first. Like Phoebe.'

'How come?'

Clemmie and I get thick. We shut the door and play doctor-doctor.

'Let's piss on the floor.' Clemmie has taken off her pants. So we do it right there behind the piano that May plays in the evenings. Right there in May's sitting room with the fragrant sweet peas in the brass flower vase. The floor shines brighter with our piss.

'Run. Run.'

And all the time I am running with Clemmie, Addy is following behind. 'Go away. You can't be in our secrets. Go!'

Then Addy falls on the stones. I see her falling down. But Clemmie has closed the door behind us already.

When I get back home Addy is sitting with Ma and applying Vaseline on her knee. 'Why didn't you let Addy play with you?'

Our kitchen is not like May's. Ma says we aren't like Khasi folk, so we don't have the fire in our kitchen like May and our pots don't shine like theirs. May makes Clemmie scrub the pots with *kwai* skin and they gleam brightly in May's dark kitchen. But our kerosene stove is blue and our pots don't shine.

Ma is making hard little sweet things to fight the sourness my father brought into her life.

'I told stupid Clemmie to let Addy...'

'Are you feeling sorry now?' Ma puts the hard little sweet things in a glossy jar.

I want to undo Addy's fall.

'Addy is accident-prone,' Ma had said once upon a time after Addy had been fished out of the water into which she had fallen.

'She's gone. She's gone...' Ma had cried before Addy had been fished out. But I knew Addy was sleeping deep in the water. Sleeping and turning green. Then there was the time Addy, her nose in a book, had walked into a glass door.

And finally she had fallen on the stones.

Addy limps to the shelf where the hard little sweet things are kept. She arches her upright little back and reaches for the hard sweet horrors that lie hiding in the places where the cobwebs sit and the lizards shit and the grim bulb casts a sulky light on all things hard and wonderful, all creatures great and small.

I buy her bubblegum to make up.

'You can't undo what you did,' Addy says. But she makes a big bubble and holds it for eight... nine... ten seconds. It doesn't burst on her face like Phoebe's did. Phoebe had a web on her face when her bubble burst and it wouldn't come off until Sissy Kay brought the cracking ice tray and Phoebe scooped up the ice cubes and rubbed and nearly scrubbed her face off.

4. MEANWHILE...

Meanwhile, in the To-Let House, Ma is waiting. She does not know why but she is waiting to spy him in the street, waiting to remember.

She remembers how it had taken her many years to discover that he could defend anything, how she had lived through each year of their life together on the idea of marriage he held out to her.

'I am not offering marriage for the world, nor the kind of marriage the world dreams of. I am talking about vows and vocations here.'

A year after Di was born the question of marriage came up again, but this time it was: 'No marriage but vows, up yours to the world by making it confront our situation; we shall be Bonnie and Clyde.'

When the girls were five and six he had read a poem. It was by Gregory Corso and yes, it was called 'Marriage.'

Finally, when half crazily she told him she could no longer live in sin though she had been doing so for a good ten years, he suggested she consult a priest, preferably a faggot. As an aside, he added that he couldn't marry her just yet for he had been married a long time ago to a woman in the city. He had neither married her for the world nor had he thrown a party for it. He had thrown up straight after the wedding was over. 'Let's hope,' he concluded, 'you don't expect that too.'

And so Ma is waiting. Learning to eat one meal a day and wait. Waiting for May to send her high-heeled sandals that fit.

We hold the sandals by the straps like dead dangling rats and race through the hedge while Kulay charges behind us with his whip screaming:

> Copycats killed the rats, Sunday morning, eat the rats.

Meanwhile, we are hard at work in May's rice fields. May's rice fields are stretches of red rice piled on cane mats spread out on the kitchen floor, where idle children are subjected to the severest labour. The mites work, in their wee wisdom, separating the chaff from the grain.

One worker, however, throws the grain and separates the chaff. Kulay

—the worker who works the hardest; who is made to chop the wood and scrub the floors and dig the soil and chop the wood and dig the soil again when he finishes; who has no rights, only duties. Kulay. Governor enters May's labour camp preceded by his white booze breath.

'*Kiad Khor Lieh...*' Kulay murmurs from his suffering spot. He has buried his hand under the pile of rice and raises it to let the lonesome grains dribble down into the pile again.

'White booze,' says Governor the connoisseur of liquors, feeling obliged to interpret the wicked smell. He creeps towards us, wearing the red jacket he washed with a hose.

'I'm going to stand guard...'

We feel the goose flesh make its appearance on our skins for it seems to us, from Governor's tone, that the end of the world is nigh and surely, surely tonight we will certainly die.

'I'm going to stand guard at the back of the house,' whispers the fiend. 'And there's a cock coming to tell me things... a great huge bloody big cock.'

And so he raves for a full week whenever we enter the kitchen to do the housework, which has to be done before we can get on with our homework.

And so he continues until May clandestinely descends upon him one night, holding a broom behind her back, and thwack-thwacks the terror out of the teller of tales.

> *Thwack-thwack... get out,*
> *Thwack-thwack... get out,*
> *Thwack-thwack... get out of town.*

But Governor still terrifies us as we crawl about May's labour camp. He still torments us in the evenings when we crawl about shutting the winking windows of the mansion. Shutting them against the weather or the Witch, we don't know which... but we never shut Governor's window. We never shut it up.

Governor's room is in the backwaters of the mansion, beyond May's imperial chambers. In the dead of the night, I dream of ghosts entering the room when the lights are out but the fire is in, and Governor's green guitar sits plucking itself, for it is actually a great big ghostly cock fleecing its own feathers to feed the wild, fiendish fires.

Meanwhile, Kulay has climbed the highest branches of the plum tree again. He spies a procession going past the mansion. Members of the Students' Union are holding blue and white flags high above their heads. Kulay stretches himself to his utmost limit and tries to touch the banners as they pass below him.

'Oust the outsiders,' shouts a band of young boys he immediately recognises from school. He has never spoken to them before. He wishes he could join them. He wishes he could run away.

> My *father is a butcher,*
> My *mother is a thief*
> Baby's in the cradle fast asleep...

Addy is breathless from skipping to the rhyme.

Clemmie and I wait patiently for our turn, when it comes.

If it comes.

Meanwhile, many things are being smuggled across the forget-me-not hedge.

Like May's discarded sunglasses for Ma to put on when she high-heels to office. The same that Clemmie wore to disguise herself from May. The very same.

'Disguise-disguise,' says Clemmie, the hot-cross bun, trying to hide behind the oversized sunglasses that cover up her fat little freckled face.

'Disguise-disguise,' repeat Addy and Di like dutiful drumsticks trying to escape from the wrath of the work-alcoholic Witch.

May gets drunk by 7 p.m.

'On the dot,' Addy adds, after several days of observation. 'Seven p.m. on di dot.'

'Aieeeee Cleeee,' screams a drunken May, drowning Clemmie's whispers.

'Who is this woman?' squeak the Bold Sunglasses blinded by the darkness inside the mansion. 'Whoever is this woman,' they squeak, as they fall off her nose and clatter to the ground, while the shrewd woman with lovely lethal eyes that dart or disappear, depending on the time of the day, destroys the disguise that dares defy her.

'Give them to your Ma,' May says picking up the dubious disguise. 'Give them to your Ma—I haf no mony.'

'Addy,' Clemmie trails behind us as we make for the To-Let House. 'Addy...'

'What?'

'Where's the dot?'

Meanwhile, Ma has hidden herself amidst the bamboo trees and is spying on the street. The procession that passed Kulay now goes past the lane that runs outside the To-Let House. People are shouting slogans. She spies a man carrying a placard that says: PROTEST! SPEAK OUT! OUST THE OUTSIDERS!

She stands there staring at the words, a little stunned. She feels the feet of the crowd trample over her, their hands clutch her throat urging her to speak. She moves her mouth to say something, but no words come.

Tears trickle down her cheek. She snaps the green bamboo stems and stuffs the broken sticks into her bag.

Meanwhile, the smuggled goods flow unchecked and Ma returning home from office says nothing about the sticks in her bag

Until...

She finds Addy the scientist, busy with a wee-wise experiment. Addy tucks her abundant hair behind her ears and pushes up the smuggled sunglasses that are falling off her nose. She soaks her smelly white socks in a grim iron bucket. Then she brings out a piece of precious pink soap smuggled from across the hedge. Smuggled from May's imperial toilet, where the silvery tap looked at the little smuggler and shook its shiny head and said: 'Shank'.

Probably thank with a stolen 'T'. Probably 'S' for 'Stolen'.

Probably wants me to thank it, thought the smuggler in her haste.

She goes scrub-scrub-rub in the water. Scrub. Scrub. Rub.

Until...

The smelly socks turn red in the face from being rubbed so hard. Until they turn red and then they turn pink.

Until...

Ma sees the scientific spectacle, scurrying around in pink socks.

Ma brings out her bamboo sticks and hits Addy on the calves.

Once. Thwack.
Twice. Thwack-thwack.
Thwack-thwack—get out of town.

Addy stands patiently while the pink socks melt like ice cream all the way down to her ankles.

Ma, seeing that the bespectacled scientist has not succumbed to her beating, snatches the sunglasses and puts them on to disguise her grief.

Perhaps, thus disguised, she will go out and try to search for him. Perhaps, thus disguised, she will try to start her life again.

5. TO START AT THE START

To start at the start is to start with cross purposes and contradictions.

To start at the start is to take the opposite directions that Ma and he are taking out of their humble home in Iewper, a day before the To-Let tenancy. For his destination is to the left of the road, where Redcoat runs Solomon's Mines, one of the many small kiosks at the foot of the mansion.

And hers is to the right.

Left. Left. Left-Right-Left.

Di and Addy march along with their mother, dressed in identical clothes.

Ma arrives at the town's only library. The ten o'clock siren has just burst through the air and two large charcoal *chulahs* stand smoking in the cold corridors before they can be carried inside to warm the stony building.

As soon as the grim double doors open, Ma pushes Addy and Di into the Children's Section on the ground floor of the library and ascends the wide staircase until she reaches the Reference Section at the top.

'Now we are six,' says Addy nostalgically, continuing, like Elizabeth Ann, to find out how God began.

> *Elizabeth Ann*
> *Had a wonderful plan*
> *She would run round the world till she found a man*
> *Who knew exactly how God began.*

Ma, in the meantime, has slipped out through an exit at the back of the library. She has returned to their home and hastily packed her things. Now, she thinks, I shall hide and he shall seek. She has no idea how long she might have to hide, but she is convinced it will not be forever. She is sure he will eventually search for her, for though their relationship is certainly a game now, she knows he cannot play it forever. She eagerly scribbles a postbox number, for she has no doubt he will look for her if she hides herself away.

Perhaps a search party will be despatched that very evening. Perhaps a repentant man will, upon finding the one-time love of his life gone missing, swear undying love if only she be returned to him. Perhaps he will fall to his knees and beg her to give him a chance to start again.

To start at the start is to start with men who burn like the blackest pieces of coal they mine up there in the hills. Men in long hair and patched pantaloons with two red sparks for eyes, where the local liquor sparks the feral imagination. Men with red-checked shirts that expose the brazen chests that resist a biblical buttoning-up. Chests that cough up the centuries-old Christian endeavour and spit it out.

In short, the chests of men like Governor.

Men like 'Governaar,' as they called him back in Quinine, his village at the end of a gorge from where he had ascended, up the unforgiving slopes, carrying a fifty-kilo rice sack on his back.

His ancestors were passionate priests and fiery warriors. Governor paled in comparison though he still went to festivals in the village where he was treated with some respect and credited with some learning, thanks to his lineage.

His was an odd family, his mother having turned to Jesus, soon after his birth. This she did primarily to find solace, for she had been deserted by her husband. The union had been so lax that it could hardly have been called 'marriage', and then it came unstuck.

Governor had a gruelling childhood, for responsibilities fell upon him thick and fast. He had taken it upon himself to bring speedy justice to his mother. He had worn his seven-league boots early in life and strode, in vain, across faraway lands in search of the scoundrel who had fathered him. He had slaughtered cows and suffocated pigs and tilled the land. He learnt chants that seduced the spirits of the dead and he could outdo any village hunk in the art of the arrow.

In his late adolescence, he broke out of this vicious cycle and decided to move townwards to get an urban whiff of things. In Shillong, he went to ProTech, the school that was a leader in vocational education. There he learnt to tailor 'the truth,' as he bragged, 'tailor the truth and iron out the ironies,' and learnt that the right to dress (and undress) people was his professional right—a fortuitous occupational perk.

If Governor and May ever exchanged stories about their youth (and they did in the first moments of love or the semblance of it), they would have had wildly different stories to tell each other.

For May, the well-bred youngest daughter of Hilarious L, had gone to the Christian Mission Girls High School where she learnt all about lace curtains and Christian hymns and polished pianos.

All of which would take a beating once Governor loomed large on her horizon.

'That half-bred, under-fed piece of inadvertent shit,' Hilarious L had thundered.

For Governor, having trained at ProTech as a tailor, was measuring up and sizing down all the young women of the locality.

'Including my daughter,' raged Hilarious L.

'Chastened her chastity,' Governor would later stamp his feet and roar in May's kitchen recounting the story of how 'Governaar,' the bare-chested heathen, had seduced the dainty daughter of a Christian cat.

'Hilarious!' Governor would clutch his drunken sides and roar, 'Hilarious father-in-law.' And he thenceforth referred to his dead father-in-law every time anything ever amused him.

To start at the start is to start with the opposite directions that Kulay and Kay take to school each morning.

For Kulay's school is down the road to the left of the mansion. And Sissy Kay's is to the right.

Left. Left. Left-Right-Left.

When Kulay arrives panting at the gates of St. James, the morning march past has begun. He has raced down the road and waded through the traffic in the rush hour of an early June morning. His striped sky-blue tie sits askew on his skinny shoulders shrunken under the weight of worrisome class Seven wisdom.

His laces are unknotted, but he is not thinking about his shoes. At least not the ones in which he has arrived. They are leaning to one side while his feet lean towards the other. He kicks at the pebbles and stones in his haste.

He is indignant because there are too many Fizzy Burps fouling the air. Too many. And because Sissy Kay has gone in the opposite direction to Bernard's where there are no marching orders. Only a voice that greets Sissy Kay's brightly shining shoes as they step onto the polished wooden floors of an airy class eight room. A deep-throated voice with a mildly sarcastic strain.

'I rather like the way you've strolled in...' says the voice, in response to Sissy Kay's girly-gruff, 'Good morning, Sir... may I enter?'

Sweating in the midst of the marching rank and file on the St. James grounds, Kulay hears in his mind's ear this brief exchange and sweats an extra drop of sweat in silent anger.

Because Bernard's is a better, bigger school to be in. He cannot comprehend why he has been sent to St James where students fight with teachers and teachers fight with one another to make their stay worthwhile. He cannot comprehend why he has to settle for second best every time. He is angry at his corner in the mansion, at the hard homework assigned to him, which has nothing to do with numbers or words but everything to do with rice, firewood and watering flowers.

Sweating under the secondary standard, Kulay believes the inferno he now finds himself in is the doing of none other than the cunning cut-throats, May and Governor.

To start at the start is to start with Governor and May on their way to a village in the south of Shillong.

Governor is seated inside a black Ambassador car and May, in her silken finery, sits beside him. Governor glances at her from time to time but she stares straight ahead.

She is staring at the vehicle in front of her.

MLO/9723, a jaded jeep, carries her elder sister Margaret M, the mother of Sissy Kay and Phoebe. Margaret M's husband is at the wheel.

This is a year before the year of the To-Let tenancy.

May is thinking about her obligation to share a part of her huge Hilarious property with her elder sister. She is thinking about which part and thinking perhaps the To-Let part. For, Margaret M is a wretched alcoholic and wouldn't notice anyway. Damien D, her husband at the wheel, is a wretched-er alcoholic and wouldn't notice anyway. Governor, driving drunkenly by her side, is the wretched-est alcoholic and wouldn't notice anyway.

They pass the village of Myl. Governor rolls down his window and barks out at his blacksmith cronies.

Mist enters the unrolled window. The jeep jitters as it begins its dangerous drive along the rim of the savage gorges. Back inside the Ambassador, Governor accelerates recklessly, speeding through his childhood haunts.

Leaving the blacksmiths in their forges, Governor drives on, unmindful of the bottomless pits hurtling a thousand miles into irretrievable memory. On and on, the drunken drivers drive, on and on. On and on and on and off...

Off, off, off the grim rim and down, down, down the devouring gorge goes the jeep, bouncing and jumping into the greedy gut of death.

'MLO/9723,' Governor says a few days later getting out of the Ambassador he was driving the day of Damien D's death.

May and a few distant relatives, relatively distant to feel any real grief, follow him and stand looking down the gorge for the sunken jeep. The gorge yawns greedily.

May sheds a couple of crocodile tears. After a hasty prayer service, Governor, by virtue of his Herculean hands, is chosen to cast a crudely crafted wooden cross across the heights.

He does so with a deafening curse.

'Damn the Devil, Delirious Ding-Dong,' he cries, getting the name of his brother-in-law all wrong. 'Damn the Devil who struck you dead.'

To start at the start is to start with a four-poster bed in the mansion, where a sixteen-year-old slumber is struck by an alarm clock.

Beep-beep
Deep-deep
Jeep-jeep
Weep-weep

Phoebe awakes, like Sleeping Beauty, and rubs her eyes.

Phoebe. A fairy and an elf.

She shall wake up like this often. After all she has become an orphan.

To start at the start is to spy him sneaking into their humble home in Iewper and surveying the considerably reduced house that Ma has left behind. The fragrance of warm chapattis from the neighbour's kitchen makes him think of her. He crumples the note she has left him and steps outside. He finishes his cigarette and goes back inside shutting the door on their life together for the last time.

P.S.: To start at the start is to never actually start.

6. A VISITOR ARRIVES AT THE MANSION

One day a visitor arrives at the mansion.

A storm.

A storm which crushes out the sun; which swirls the leaves in gay abandon and brings the small oranges to the ground; which tickles the tall, slender bamboo trees until they bend to the limits of their tickling sides and beg, 'Please stop! Storm! Please stop.'

It is only dawn but the storm is hungry for havoc. By the time it arrives at the mansion, it has eaten a good many rooftops of churches and schools and killed a hundred villagers.

Governor, looking out of his still dark window, receives this piece of news with vindication.

'Ha! Ha! Serves them right,' he laughs. But the storm rattles up a great many thoughts in his head. He hears the faint rattling of a tiny tin roof stretched above a tiny Governor head. The storm carries him back to a thin little hut made from flattened kerosene tins back there in Quinine, his vertical village. The tinned roof is smeared with thick black coal tar. Four rounded boulders on its edges hold the roof from flying away.

He throws himself on the bed and allows the storm to come in through his window and get on top of him. It skims his bare chest and glides along his taut veins. Then it moves up and licks his face getting into the crevices around his puckered eyes, leaving grit in his hair. His nostrils begin to dilate with disparate odours. The odour of smoky, coal-tarred roofs. The odour of riding piggyback inside his brother's, EverComfortSon's, conical basket as they raced through meandering orange groves covering great distances in hungry strides. He liked to think of his brother, Edward, as EverComfortSon because of the great comfort their mother derived from her elder child.

'As thy days, so shall thy strength be...' he mutters lazily, closing his eyes and thinking of the torch-lit, tarred shed of his childhood throbbing with the evening cicadas. He lies waterlogged, like the ripened paddy crop EverComfortSon refrained from harvesting on Sundays. Nor, for that matter, would he sit at the family's wooden meat shop at Iewduh market calling 'original boneless beef...' on that holy day of God.

'Spineless,' Governor mutters. '(Never)ComfortSon the bastard,' he swears, for his frugal family never did him any good.

His dangling hand tightens around a bottle of rice beer lurking beneath his bed. Curiosity-the-cat, May's green-eyed cat, who is under the bed, scurries away in fright at the sight of a calloused hand dancing in the dark.

'Curiosity-the-cat has sucked before I did,' Governor roars, rising again with the darkening clouds and holding up the half-empty bottle. 'Kulay the Rat has drunk before I did.'

He empties the bottle into his sarcastic mouth. Through the rain-lashed window, he spies Redcoat hurrying towards the garage for shelter from the storm. He lets out a low whistle.

She retreats further into the garage, pretending not to have heard him. Unable to see her anymore, he shuts the window and returns to his bed.

And there he lies in wait, knowing from the depths of his crippled liver that he was born for higher things. The thought will eventually compel him to leap up and grab his green guitar. He will strum stories that creep towards the limelight, he imagines, lurking in the eyes of the enchanted children.

But for now he is liquor-logged and quiet. Quite drunk.

Then the storm turns the world red,
Then it turns the world yellow,
And then it decides that the world,
Shall be simultaneously murderous and mellow.

Kulay's indigo-blue kite flies higher than any kite has before. It soars gaily into the dark grey sky even while sunlight slyly dapples the leaves of May's enormous India rubber tree. The tree has, over the years, got mixed up with the wraith-like weeping willow and now embraces it with a forget-me-not tenacity.

'A misty moisty morning... most certainly,' says May staring, according to her old hangover habit, out of the parlour window while she unsuccessfully tries to free herself from Governor's tentacles.

'Misty-moisty' represents for May two ends of a spectrum, which encompass between them all the shades and hues of Shillong's whimsical weather.

May, being particularly absent-minded this morning, hasn't noticed exactly when Governor strayed into the parlour. She is rubbing her teeth viciously with a piece of kwai skin and thinking of Sissy Kay's deep-voiced and mildly sarcastic teacher, Benjamin.

Her meandering thoughts begin with her opening the window to gaze upon the weather and the world. Pungent smoke from smouldering rubber hits her whisky-smothered throat. The smell is emanating from the tyres the Union boys are burning in the field to protest against exploitation by the dkhars. Inside the mansion, the odours merge with the smell of the beedis that Governor gets free of cost from Solomon's Mines. The fumes, entering May's throat via her delicate pearl-drop nostrils, bring up tears in her eyes and hurt her throat. She decides there and then that she hates the world. She crosses herself at the thought but feels justified in having had it.

'After all, I've been mistreated,' she says to no one in particular (and certainly not to Governor). 'I've been mistreated by Hilarious L and his wife... my mother...'

'Shit luck, May,' Governor offers anyway.

One memory that still brings tears to her eyes is that of the hospital, housed in a sprawling bungalow.

She remembers herself at sixteen suffering from a severe tonsillitis condition. She remembers lying on her white bed, staring out of the hospital window, waiting for a visit from a well-wisher. She could see colossal columns of smoke rising from the chimney opposite her, threatening to lift the entire hospital by the skin of its teeth and send it swirling into the sky.

No well-wisher had come. Neither Hilarious L nor his wife, Sara Sooting. Neither Margaret M nor Damien D.

May swallowed hard and her tonsils hurt harder. She stared out at the cloud-capped promontory, visible against the blackened sky, with a growing premonition that she was going to die. Her infection was not just limited to her throat but had developed in the lymph nodes high up in her neck. It had spread into the soft tissues about the tonsils and formed an abscess. All this had been explained to her by Dr Hurler as she lay sweating in a terrible fever.

She was certain that Hilarious and his flighty wife were hobnobbing with government top brass in raucous revelry while she lay on her deathbed, beside herself with rage.

At school, she had turned into a wilful child and the teachers sent across notes complaining of her misdemeanours. She was often found in 'Truth Tailors,' the tailoring shop Governor had opened across from the Christian Mission Girls High School for the sheer visual benefits he derived by being so strategically located.

As May succumbed to general anaesthesia, she was certain that she would die unloved. She had suffered the indignities of blood and urine tests alone and decided, at the exact point that the syringe pierced her transparent skin, that she loathed the world and those who had carelessly brought her into it.

The ignorant nurse who was carefully wheeling May on a trolley towards the Operation Theatre had no idea that when she came to, the patient would have had two things out of her system. One was her tonsils. The other was her heart.

'Shit luck, wife,' Governor offers again, bringing May back from her reverie into the present day parlour.

May bites his hand viciously.

But the devil is feeling particularly devilish this day for he has concluded a splendid game of archery just the previous evening. He is still dressed in a sea-green shirt and the broad-brimmed cowboy hat that he picked up from the Over Bridge (OB) – the thriving black market suspended over Iewduh – where cackling women sold piles of clothes sent as charity from richer countries.

'What will a poor man do with a hat?' Governor asked, picking it up with the hooked end of a snake-shaped stick.

The hat dangled from it like a huge baited fish. 'I shan't buy this hat if you can answer that,' repeated Governor amidst the cacophony of the black bazaar. When no one could or cared to answer him, Governor donned the hat and was about to walk away without paying.

But,

> There were two big bullies at the door, door, door,
> They caught him by the collar,
> And they made him pay a dollar,
> And he didn't go to OB any more, more, more.

Governor jigs about in his black market costume recalling with pleasure the events of the previous day, when the hopes of millions of enthusiasts were pinned on him as they thronged the *thoh teem* kiosks all over town and gambled on the number of arrows that would be shot by players from different localities in Shillong.

By the time the players assembled in the low-lying field stretched out under a stand of conifers, where wide-eyed snotty boys would search for pennies in the next day's dawn, Governor had donned his smuggled hat and got out his special bamboo bow and gut. He commanded that the finest arrows of special reed with peacock feathers on their necks and metal caps on their tips be brought before him.

> And he stood there in his Levis imitations,
> And he stood there in his hat
> And he stood there in the setting sun
> And he said, 'I'm a kinda wild cat.'

He was sweating a great deal by this time. 'I'm a kinda furless pussy... y'know,' he told the crowds pressing behind him, wanting to catch a glimpse of the giant at his sport.

He was trying to concentrate on the circular grassy target, thirty metres away. It was attached to a thin bamboo pole.

'Over the notch... Governor, over the notch my son...' he mumbled to himself, for any arrow hitting below the notch would not fetch any points.

Fifteen hundred arrows had been showered in four minutes. As the news spread, it was learnt that the maximum arrows shot were Governor's elegant, purple-feathered ones. Governor took off his hat and bowed to the adoring audience. 'Life is a gamble,' he began, beaming—

> Politics is a scramble...
> I am William Tell...
> And you can go to Hell...

Lewd shouts burst through the darkening conifers as torches were lit and the loudest drunken dancing ensued.

'Shish-ish-ish,' shivered Reverend Ontheway, as he tried to make his way to the Presbyterian Church amidst the somersaulting sinners who had drowned themselves in cheap liquor.

As the revellers lunged forward into the torch-lit night they would only be rivalled by Reverend Ontheway's sermon that came to them on amplified waves and which they tried hard to stop from entering their ears.

Governor is still reeling under the effect of that demonic dance as he prances in the parlour, which is why he dares prod May here and there until she yells in disgust, 'Wash the car, Governor. Wash the car. We haf no mony.'

The car she refers to isn't the Aston Martin but the ramshackle Ambassador they have kept locked up in the garage since the day of Damien D's death. May has 'mony' on her mind for she wants to convert the car into a taxi at the earliest.

Governor has been unsuccessfully trying to negotiate a lease of the car for sometime now.

'I've been cooking for twenty years,' says May, crushing a betel leaf into her mouth and surreptitiously rubbing the lime paste from it behind a flowerpot of honey-orange orchids that decorate the window sill.

She observes that the fragile things are doing well in the peat she has asked Ma to smuggle from the Conservation Centre. The flowers arch themselves up on tentative green stems quite in the manner that a new love-shaped heart is beginning to tremble within May's breast. Outwardly, however, she still sticks to her weather-beaten dull green sweater, fraying at the cuffs and held together by a silvery safety pin.

May first spotted Benjamin in Golf Links last month, when a mid-summer breeze was blowing through his wavy hair despite the red baseball cap that did its best to keep all passion in place. May, who was speeding past the golf course in her lunatic vehicle, threw caution to the divine summer breeze and submitted with gay abandon to the charms that his expensive (and most definitely foreign) sunglasses reflected.

'After all, I've been mistreated,' muttered May as she went about town trying to gather every little titbit of information that could possibly be gathered under a sceptical Shillong sun.

Her informants told her:

That his name was Benjamin Budoor.

That he adored Belo, the Alsatian thoroughbred that accompanied him on his walks through Bernard's.

That he was a versatile musician because he played, in addition to the violin, the piano (here May's heart took a little leap), the trumpet, the trombone, the flute and the guitar.

That he was a gardener. At this May's joy knew no bounds and she decided there and then the exact number of cuttings and bulbs she would give him on their second meeting, for the first must be left to test the waters.

May then approached him on the pretext of inquiring after Sissy Kay's academic performance and had very soon left an indelible impression on the man. He worried if he had been charming enough, for it still gave him a bit of a shock when women crossed the threshold of his school.

May is brought sharply back from her romantic musings by the sound of Governor thrashing at the asters with a leather strap outside. The demon hasn't quite died in him and he is looking for more avenues of amusement.

The storm appears to agree with his sentiments for it rumbles like a hungry ogre's stomach announcing its gluttonous intent.

'Governaar...,' May screams, but he lashes out with the strap for he knows of her latest betrayal in an oblique kind of way and decides to likewise thrash her obliquely by thrashing her flowers.

And so, applauded by the storm, he goes, with an impotent rage, at the purple and pink blossoms trembling on their green stalks declaring, 'We all hate you! Hate! Hate! Hate!'

Governor explodes with jealously and anger at having to slave about the house while May conducts her affairs. He feels very much like a metal-tipped arrow ready to pierce the skin of things and rip them apart. Entering again through the parlour window, he grabs May roughly and bangs her head on the piano.

Clang.
Clang.
Clang.

Then he rushes out again to attack the fragrant flowers and the sticks that prop them up until they come crumbling down onto the damp earth May has softened with her spade.

'You swearing, drunken dog. You know I call a spade a spade,' May screams, certain in the knowledge that she is worth much more than her crude and cruel husband. She bangs the doors and windows of the mansion shut against the monster and the storm.

Governor thrashes the asters for a bit more, hoping to tear through the tender tissues. He tries to recall Kiyahoi, the A-Siamese tenant, lashing at his Finnish wife, but realises that whereas the former had a real woman to receive his whip, he only has a frail apology. He thrashes hard and the smell of the green grass and the wild wilderness rushes into his nostrils and dilates them.

The storm regains its tempo and appears to be progressing parallel to the one that is raging inside his breast. He lets out a muffled cry and compares it to that of the pigs Evercomfortson suffocates for a living.

'I sound worse than a suffering swine,' says Governor, 'and what's more... I need a real woomaan... Hilarious! Hilarious father-in-law!'

Meanwhile Kulay's indigo-blue kite is sailing in a funny-coloured sky. He can hear Governor and May quarrelling inside the mansion. He wishes the cunning cut-throats would cut each other's throats and be done with it. That would bring him the freedom he craves for—the freedom to fly, like his kite, in a funny-coloured sky.

'A funny fair-is-foul, foul-is-fair kind of sky,' says May, finally shutting herself inside Hilarious L's wooden library at the far end of the mansion. May jealously guards the entrance to the library for she believes herself to be the sole inheritor of all knowledge that exists in the house.

> *When shall we meet again?*
> *In thunder, lightning or in rain?*

She sighs, picking up Hilarious L's hardboiled copy of *Macbeth* and settling comfortably inside the skin of the first witch. She imagines she hears Benjamin's dog, Belo, barking but it is only Curiosity-the-cat meowing in a mulish kind of way.

'Kill the swine,' May mutters, for the sound of Governor's rage is hitting the centre of her head and throwing it into turmoil.

The wind changes its mind and so does Kulay's indigo-blue kite.

Two solemn heads sit on the steps of the porch watching the saga in the sky and pondering on some points to ponder.

'What's shik-shik?' I ask Clemmie.

We are sitting on the stone steps and it is grey like the end of the world.

May has told us about the end of the world when we will all meet each other without our clothes – even the dead people – and we'll sit on the weighing scale to see if our good deeds are weightier than the bad. Then we'll proceed either to heaven or to hell where our bums are waiting to be burnt for all our sins.

'Clemmie, what's shik-shik?'

'What Governor does to May at night.' Clemmie is huddled in Phoebe's secret shawl.

'What?'

'Spy-spy and then you'll know.'

'Tell me.'

'You get babies after it.'

'How?'

'From your bum.'

And we talk for a long time about May and Governor and wonder how things will be if we went to heaven instead.

'But we'll never go.'

'Why?'

'Because we talked about shik-shik.'

'So?'

'Shik-shik is sin.'

'Then the babies? They are also sin?'

'No.'

'So?'

'So what—kiss the pot.'

Governor is walking about with the aim of finding a real woman to wreak his wrath on when he hears Clemmie screaming 'Governor! Governor!'

'Governor, Governor,' she screams, and when Governor comes around, red from drinking (and shik-shik, Clemmie presumes) a pale yellow kite is going up to challenge Kulay's at *kynteng*.

'It's a Malki kite *liah*...' Kulay swears, confident because he has strengthened his kite strings with crushed glass. Governor lunges forward to grasp the string, but Kulay hisses, 'Get out dog,' and Governor grabs Clemmie and lifts her high up in the air to cover up.

'You're a kite, my girl,' he roars.

Clemmie giggles and says, 'Carry Di also, carry her also.' By the time he puts her back on the ground, May has appeared.

May's high heels go click-clock, click-clock, and we know she is angry.

'May see moi kite,' Kulay speaks funnily because May can do anything when she's angry. But it doesn't help. She is hot and cross and she pulls fiercely at the invisible kite strings until Kulay's blue kite comes fluttering into her hands. Then she looks at Governor.

'Wash the car, Governor,' May grinds her teeth. 'Wash the car—we haf no mony.'

Witnessing this vicious exchange from across the hedge is a pair of grief-stricken sunglasses. Ma's. She does not pause to push up the eye gear even though it is slipping off her sweaty nose.

The sky is beginning to grumble again. A drop of water falls off the bridge of Ma's nose. A teary raindrop.

'Smells like a storm,' says Ma, well aware of Shillong's eccentric elements. She peers through the hedge and spies Di seated on the hood of Governor's car, dangling her skinny legs in the air.

'Shillong is the Rome of the East,' Governor is telling Di. 'And I am its Romeo...'

He offers his forefinger to the girl and leads the trailing question mark towards the garage.

'Open Sim-Sim,' says the ill-meaning magician, opening the door himself.

'I could tear through the hedge...but my sari would be tattered by the thorns amidst the lavish green growth,' Ma thinks, tired of being the Good Woman of Shillong.

7. PUDDLES AND DREAMS

Addy has gone inside her book again.

'Addy. Addy. Addeeeee...'

'I can't hear when I read.'

Addy is reading the story of Paws the Dog for the seventh time.

'Do something useful,' Addy says, like Paws the Dog who has rescued the Big Woolly Bear from the spiteful Busy Bees. From our bedroom window I can see Governor coming out of the garage. But he is not looking at me. He is talking to Clemmie. Telling her something. Is he going to take her to the garage? I hope so. I hope he'll take her into the garage like he took me.

I tell Addy the day of the school fete. She is wearing her yellow dress with the swinging pocket purse. She looks grown-up because she is wearing glasses. Addy had taken off her glasses to cry in the morning because her white shoes had turned black. She had tried to shine them with a white liquid but they had turned black.

'It said MAGIC LIQUID on the cover,' Addy pretended something had got into her eyes because Ma was hot and cross and said she wouldn't buy any more white sports shoes.

'C'mon, c'mon, pull out a coin.' Addy is looking important. 'Pull out a coin and drop it in the bucket. Send it clinking to the one inside the water. Clinking all the way down.'

So I open my red purse with the brown lion's face and I pull out a coin and drop it into the bucket. It goes, like Addy, in the lake all the way to the bottom. But it never touches the other coin.

'It didn't touch—you don't get a prize.' The class ten girl fishes out the coin and puts it in her tin.

Addy and I walk away. The tin is heavy and singing.

'Addy!'

Addy adjusts her 'One in a Million' badge and heads towards the Lucky Dip stall.

'Addy!'

I'm trailing behind my big sister trying to tell her why things are not the same anymore...

'Is it the lost coin?' Addy fishes out a one rupee coin from her red purse.

'No.'

'Then what?' She is in a hurry for Lucky Dip. 'Because you lost your purple border hanky?'

'Green border.'

'Because of that?'

'No.'

'Then what?' Addy is impatient. She pushes up her glasses. Her eyes are wide as wonder. 'What?'

And when I tell her, Addy says it's fine. It's fine for old Governor to kiss Skinny Me. But it's not like that. It's not like that at all and if I tell Addy again she won't believe me because what I told her just now will then be a lie.

Addy is sensible. She tucks her hair behind her ears and pushes up her spectacles. She wins a mini rocking chair at Lucky Dip and buys sweets for both of us.

'Shillong is the Scotland of the East... and... I am its Scot.'

Governor advances menacingly towards Addy, Clemmie and me, wrapping May's *tapmoklieh* around himself and looking like a piper of the Queen's own Cameron Highlanders in full dress. He has stolen May's choicest tartan shawl from her great wooden chest of drawers where the shawls lie neatly folded one upon the other.

Clemmie is busy splashing about in the puddles that the storm has left behind.

'It's the storm that made them, Mujupeas,' Phoebe calls out. She is standing at May's kitchen door wearing a blue, checked tablecloth over her jeans. She calls it *jainkersha*. We know she's about to wash her sports uniform because the sun is out today.

Meanwhile we walk in the puddles—Addy, Clemmie and I. Clemmie jumps hard on the little pools of water and they burst on our clothes.

'There'll be no puddles in the lake, no?'

'The lake is a giant puddle.' Addy is writing poems these days.

Clemmie comes near us and jumps again. There is a rainbow in the water.

'How come Addy? How come?'

'Someone coloured the puddle with crayons.'

'Who? How come?'

'No,' Addy thoughtfully mixes the puddle with her finger. 'I've seen it before. After it rains.'

Clemmie stamps on the coloured water again and we are wet. So wet.

'Say sorry,' Addy scolds.

'Sorry.'

'But sorry doesn't make a dead man alive.'

The colour is gone from the water and May is calling because it's time for the Witch.

Ignoring May's screams, we stand over Phoebe as she washes her clothes near the tap behind the garage. She has tied back her hair with a red ribbon.

'The clothes still look dirty even when they are washed, no?'

'They'll look clean when they dry.' Phoebe is scrubbing in the soapy water with her white fairy hands.

Sissy Kay stands in his favourite place in front of the garage. It is open and there is no car inside. His face is an about-to-cry red.

'Eat my socks,' he screeches. 'I challenge you devils to eat my socks.'

'He's trying to act like Kulay,' Clemmie whispers in my ear trying to make up for splashing in the puddles and making us wet.

I want to eat Sissy Kay's sweaty green socks. I munch on them but they taste only like sweaty green socks. When I take them out of my mouth, he says,

'Two boys tried to drown me in the lake... *dkhar* boys.'

'That's why you're acting tough with girls?' Clemmie puts on Kulay's bullying tone.

'What did you do, Sissy Kay?' I want to know.

'I hugged them.'

'Then?'

'Then Kulay saw me and he charged full speed.'

'Then?'

'Then they got scared and ran.'

'Don't lie.' Clemmie says. 'Don't tell lies.'

Suddenly May marches up to us. Her blouse is nearly coming off.

Clemmie goes red. 'Don't tell,' she tries to turn away. 'Don't tell anyone you saw her like that.'

May grabs Clemmie by the neck.

'Time for your piano lessons, my girl.' They both go in and May stomps on the piano.

'Go home.' Phoebe splashes the dirty clothes' water and the tin basin clangs like May's piano. 'Go home. May is drunk.'

May gets drunk that day like never before. It is already dark when the piano stops playing and the crashing of plates replaces it.

Addy is tight-lipped.

'It's those blue-and-white plates.' Addy purses her lips as Ma says it is bad to interfere in other people's lives.

All night long May smashes the blue-and-white plates that brighten her dark kitchen. I know Clemmie is hiding with her brother Kulay. Hiding and crying. Sissy Kay is with his big sister Phoebe. But they don't cry because May is not their mother. When May stops, everything is quiet.

In the middle of the night Ma hears Kulay screaming from bad dreams.

'It's all because of Governor and his ways.' Ma tosses away the musty-smelling quilt and gets out of bed, hitting the glass vase Kiyahoi left behind in her anger. She leans over to see if the sound has woken her dreaming daughters.

But Addy is fast asleep pursing her lips in case something slips out of her mouth in the night.

And Di is dreaming.

Dreaming she is a princess tossing and turning in her sleep. Dreaming she is lying atop forty feather mattresses stuffed with fleeced feathers from Governor's great big cock. When Di awakes, it will be Sunday. On Sunday all people become sundry.

The sundry people, standing at the foot of Di's bed, proclaim that:

The storm is over.

And that:

Di is a princess.

May is the monitor of the sundry mob. She lodges a ladder against the forty feather mattresses and lifting up her silken dress, (lest she trips on the tassels), ascends graspingly to the top. Di sits atop the feather mattresses rubbing her eyes.

Di is called Di but looks like Phoebe.

> *Did you have a good night?*
> *Did you have a good night?*
> *Did you have a good night, Jane?*

queries May, hoping against hope that the answer will be yes.

'No.'

'And why ever not?'

I turn and toss, and toss and turn, and feel I am at the bottom of the dark blue sea.

'Hurray!' yells Kulay the prince from below. 'Hurray!'

For it has been established beyond the shadow of a doubt that forty feathery mattresses weren't enough to prevent the princess from feeling the prickly-little-May-planted pea.

Therefore Di is a pure princess and Kulay, a pure prince. May, the pure Witch, descends dejectedly down the ladder.

All and sundry return to Monday.

The dream of the princess and the pea ends.

I turn over and scream. The bed is wet. Ma clamps my mouth shut.

'Give that dress to Charity,' she hisses.

Ma tiptoes out of one room into the only other one. Kiyahoi's trunk glimmers under its white shroud in the dark.

Who was Kiyahoi? Ma wonders, sitting herself down on the green rocking chair. Who was Kiyahoi, and why did he try to finish his Finnish wife?

Ma is not amused. It is dark and she does not switch on the light. Moonlight filters in through the un-curtained windows. It is the right time, Ma thinks, to ponder on her strategies for survival and shed a couple of tears. She is missing somebody.

Voices float up from May's row of shady shops below the mansion compound. Curiosity-the-cat mews mournfully. The cat has smelt a rat.

But it is only Ma lifting up the creaking lid of Kiyahoi's trunk and peering inside in the hope of finding the person she is missing.

Contrary to her expectations, he has not come looking for her. He has not written nor has he called. She misses his beard. Her body has a mind of its own and it decides to miss his beard.

Crouching beside the trunk, she runs her fingers through the pages of several books lying one upon the other.

When we talk about Finland we talk of a nation at the continent's extreme edge...

Ma imagines an elegant peppermint voice belonging to Kiyahoi's wife filter out of the trunk and fill the room. The voice bears no trace of domestic disgrace. It is colourful and concise.

Ma squints at the crumbling books surfacing from the trunk in yellowing hundreds.

Picking up a kerosene lamp, she slides open the bolt of the front door that leads out into the citrus garden. It moans wide open as the lady with the lamp slips through it.

She is barefoot. 'That's fine,' she thinks. Her sore, swollen feet feel the wind's caress as if he is fingering them again. She treads lightly trying not to tease the bones of things buried beneath the ground.

Borthakur is sitting in his usual place as he has done every night before this. From the distance, the sound of muffled weeping seeps through the thin walls of his home and reaches them.

'It is a husband's duty to beat his wife,' he says. 'I do my duty everyday.'

Tonight he does not tell her any stories. They sit watching the night as if they are worshipping it. The sounds of the night accompany her thoughts of the cold North Country that the Finnish woman has returned to.

Perhaps it is the salt in her tears, the level of lamplight, the chill in the air, the unblinking stars or the smell of the opium that Borthakur takes which make her eloquent.

She sits on the edge of the night reliving the first pangs of love in the velvet darkness.

At the crack of dawn, Borthakur, having heard her story and received her instructions, rouses himself from his stupor, and makes for his home. She rises and slips back into the house.

Red and yellow and pink and green
Purple and orange and blue...

Di has begun her second rainbow-in-the-puddle-dream.

When the dream turns into a scream, Ma clamps my mouth shut and insists again that we give the dress to Charity.

8. SUNKEN SECRETS

Governor piles us into the big black Ambassador, which May has ordered should be turned into a taxi at the earliest, and takes us to Watts Lake to feed the fish and have 'a happy family time,' as he says showing us his *kwai*-stained teeth to match his red, drunken eyes.

It is a lazy, summer Sunday afternoon and we sit in his black car and go to the lake.

Addy carries her plastic blue toy fish and Clemmie carries popcorn. Governor gives me the Jim Reeves cassette cover to hold and we sing 'Rail road, steam boat, river and canal...' as we go driving past the fire brigade building, where Borthakur bends double as Governor honks at him, past our school where we shout, 'school-school,' past Kulay's school where he swears loudly and tries to throw stones if he has any.

When we arrive, the lake is green and there are red and yellow boats in it.

'Full of *Khar Neps*,' Kulay swears at which Governor tries to kick him because, as Clemmie tells us, 'Khar Nep' means Nepalis and Governor has many friends among them.

Addy dips her toy fish in and out of the water.

'It's happy now,' Addy says.

'How do you know?'

'Because it's not a fish out of water.'

Clemmie drops the popcorn into the water and the fish come floating up.

'There, there, I saw the orange one.'

We lean on the white wooden bridge and the fish come up to eat Clemmie's popcorn. Then Clemmie drops the empty packet of popcorn into the lake too.

'Never do that. You'll kill the fish.'

Governor crooks his finger and we follow him meekly to the grassy slopes. Kulay goes off to chase the kites and bully the kite-fliers. We sit around Governor who tells us the story of Watts Lake.

'It's not Watts Lake, silly-billies, it's Ward's Lake.'

He tells us the story of the prisoner who dug the lake because he didn't know what to do.

'He was like Kulay the Devil.' Governor shades his eyes to look for Kulay.

'Kulay-Kulay, come back Kulay!' we scream frightened.

'Clemmie-Di!' someone sings from far away.

'There! There, he's in the trees.' Addy spies him.

When we reach home, we try to fly the deep pink kite Kulay has captured from the trees, even though it is dark.

We see Redcoat coming up the gravelled driveway, for her day's work is over. She stands staring at Kulay's kite until he barks out at her. She withdraws into the tenant quarters. After a while, we see Governor slinking out of the mansion and disappearing in the direction that Redcoat has just gone.

Inside the mansion, May is drawing the orange curtains.

Suddenly, everything turns silent as if something is about to happen.

The 'happy family' has, on this visit to Ward's Lake, seen something out of the corner of their eyes that none of them dares to speak about.

Sissy Kay lies in bed and tosses this way and that. He is sad that he will never hear the whole world fart at one go. This despite the fact that Benjamin has given him a badge that makes just such a tall claim, or at least hints at the possibility. WHAT IF THE WHOLE WORLD FARTED AT ONE GO? asks the badge in bold black letters against a cheeky yellow background.

'What if... what if,' Sissy Kay thinks sleepily, though he knows that this is highly unlikely and at any rate not unanimously admissible.

Like the thing that he saw in the mansion out of the corner of his eye; the thing that he spied when no one knew he was looking; the thing he caught Governor doing, after the latter had followed Redcoat into the tenant quarters, oblivious of the fact that he was being spied upon by none other than sneaky Sissy Kay; the very thing he might yet tell May.

Like a smiling dead secret that everyone knows and no one dares to think of.

Addy is thinking about her badge too. The little tin thing. The one that says, I'M ONE IN A MILLION, and is painted like the orange inside of a pumpkin.

Addy had pinned it to the red piping of her grey pinafore and proceeded to school where she had been warned by none other than Sister Christine, the principal, that pride preceded a fall.

'Pride hath a fall, dear... uhhmm,' said Sister Christine, wagging her finger at Addy's tin thing.

Addy has hidden the badge under her pillow and is thinking of the day's events, wondering how pride could fall and if, when it fell, it had been sitting on a horse. She turns in a quiet way towards the window side of the bed and looks out at the un-curtained night with wide sleepy eyes. The lantana bushes, whose yellow and red flowers look like Mr. Gooptu's costly ten paisa sweets, have been subdued by the dark and look like poisonous blackberries. Addy's head is full of wild ideas for she has been perusing, with some seriousness, the volumes of Enid Blyton and has absorbed with alacrity the possibility of other magical planets.

She lies wide asleep, thinking of the thing she had seen out of the corner of her eye. It was a rusty orange hint of a secret and it had floated into Addy's vision as she sat listening to the story of the lake. A man in the distance had caught her attention. Addy was sure the man was her father. He had looked away just as she was about to wave out to him. He had walked rapidly towards a woman waiting for him at the entrance to the lake. Addy thought she knew the woman too, but perhaps she had made it all up. She felt her ears grow hot and red but she decided to keep the secret to herself and soon enough it had wafted out of her vision and decided to plague Governor - that teller of tales himself.

May is mulling over her own secrets when Governor returns from the lake with the children.

She sits brushing her tresses at an oblong mirror. The mirror is cracked in two so that it is only half a mirror. Half May sits brushing her tresses and gasping at herself. 'How could I be such a fool?' she asks her altered image.

She'd had a choice. In the Christmas season, when the mansion was immersed in the aroma of the season's spices, every dish gleaming, the brass glossy, the holly in place, the floors scrubbed and lustrous and the maids English-speaking, for they were Hilarious L's maids and he was a man of distinction.

May flushed by the wood stove, the wine and the songs rendered in the most incredible of voices. His name was Alders. She knew he had a secret admiration for her. A rich fool.

'He would have still been rich now. I would have been better off.'

Instead, she had married Governor to spite Hilarious L. Now that he was dead, she felt degraded by the union. She was surprised at herself. Earlier, he was her first thought the minute the mansion was empty.

'It's not everyday one gets to lie on a couch like this...'

Governor would look ridiculous in the ornate settings of the mansion, yet his misanthropic wit charmed her.

'Hilarious L might not have the last laugh yet.'

He slobbered like a wet dog and she so relished the firewater on his tongue.

But it had not lasted.

'Why the warpaint this evening, wife? Not playing the field I hope.'

'Nope.'

She waited impatiently for him to leave.

He had just returned from his village and was full of spirits. He had been called to exorcise the ghost of a pig that had got into EverComfortSon.

'Scrub the floor, Governor.'

'And where are the maids, wife?'

'I haf no maids.'

She slammed the door. The night was cool and the fire brigade was sounding the seven o'clock gong.

But what had Governor done when she banged the door on him that long-ago night?

Hadn't he crawled to the backward parts of the mansion and knocked at the door of a red-coated tenant? Hadn't he entered into a certain musty space, where the smell of fresh milk mingled with Jai Mata *beedis* and dangerously dilated his nostrils? Hadn't he asked Borthakur to be on guard? And hadn't Borthakur, taking his post at the door, put his pillow on the doormat and snored off to sleep?

Governor remembers, with a shiver that runs through his spine, how he caught the barely visible whisper of a secret, as it went floating past. He winces at the memory of a thing so slight and so ugly.

Earlier in the day, he had shut one of his roving eyes and carried on with his story of Ward's Lake, cautioning the audience to do likewise.

A bad omen in the form of a sunken boat was taking a stroll in the waters. It paused to gawk at the curious family, taunting and challenging it to come clean with its own sunken secrets.

'We have none', Governor whispered in his heart of hearts though the sunken secrets were surging through him now in an unstoppable flood. And while he stood, as was his habit, on an elevation in the ground, a great many scenes from his past floated up with the sunken boat and stared him in the face.

There he was, a man of twenty six, just married to May and full of hope, for Hilarious L had died and there was work to do. He had many plans.

'Hey Borthakur! Bastard! Get your ass here!', he bellowed, deciding to involve his fireman buddy in the execution of his splendid ideas. Little did he know that Borthakur would be the bearer of bad news—for the bastard came crawling with the rumour that May had cuckolded Governor.

That was the first time he had stealthily visited Redcoat's quarters. She was startled, but it would be wrong to say he coerced her. His grip was tight but received no resistance. He did not try to disguise his despair. Still, like the liquor, she had become his habit.

Her father, Dull Bahadur, had been Hilarious L's dutiful *daju* until one day he turned violent and threatened to destroy the mansion with a *dao*. No one knew precisely what triggered the lunacy, though it was whispered that it had something to do with his opening the doors of his own tenant quarters and stumbling upon Borthakur who was meant to be guarding the door.

Dull Bahadur charged into the mansion swearing revenge at the sight of what he had seen, but being a little unsteady in his purpose, he had tripped over Curiosity-the-cat's mother (who was taking a stroll across the parlour), fallen flat on his head, haemorrhaged, and died.

Redcoat was allowed to stay on in the quarters and run Solomon's Mines, where she sat from dawn to dusk and then returned to the mansion to complete the daily chores May allotted her. Late at night she would return to her quarters and smoke her remaining *beedis*.

'She's a Black Magic Woman,' May insisted. 'I wouldn't meddle with her.'

It was true that Redcoat was a strange, quiet woman. She wore brightly coloured clothes and exuded a dank odour. Sometimes she made little paper dolls and thrust them into the hands of the children without a single word.

Governor shrugs off the shiver and tries to sleep.

In the To-Let House, Ma stands looking at the street through the uncurtained window, hoping again to catch a glimpse of what she has been denied. Perhaps that is him dancing a strange dance and wielding a sword of feathers, she thinks. The secret she has been trying to suppress bubbles up inside her and slips out of her mouth in the form of a little burp. The barely visible burp goes floating past her, and she winces at the sight of a thing so slight and so ugly. It pauses to gawk at the unhappy woman, challenging her to come clean with her own suppressed secrets.

I have none, she whispers in her heart of hearts, for the sunken secrets are surging through her now in an unstoppable flood. And while she stands, as is her habit, at the uncurtained window, a great many scenes from her past float up with the renegade burp and decide to stare her in the face.

Let him leave.
Let him be.
Let him have wings.

This man, you shouldn't miss him, warns the buoyant burp.

She says, 'Yes,' and feels a momentary ecstasy. But a strange kind of throbbing carves out a room in her chest, making itself quite at home. She thinks of how she had sent Borthakur in search of him after he had failed to show up at the To-Let House like she had expected him to do.

Six weeks had elapsed since the day she had walked out of their home, hoping he would plead with her to return to him. But no such thing happened. She began to worry about him and her worries prompted her to send Borthakur to inquire after him. She dared not venture out herself, lest he spurn her again.

But Borthakur had disappointed her. He had been unable to trace his whereabouts. He had found their home in Iewper empty and locked. The landlord did not have a clue about where he had disappeared. He had left without paying his bills. Borthakur had nothing else to report. He stuck out his hand for the money she had promised him and disappeared into the darkness.

Standing at the window, Ma remembers how she had received this news. She had been wordless for a while. Then she strung together a couple of socially useful sounds and carried them around like a packed linguistic lunch—hurried and handy. Snapping sounds for the girls, sweeter sounds for society.

Ma now stands motionless, unable to utter a single word. She is consumed by hatred as intense as the love she had once felt for him. But she knows that sooner or later love will consume this hate again. She waits with dread to be turned inside out against her will. A distant scream shatters the silence. She feels strangely akin to Kulay who is screaming in his sleep again.

Kulay has been awoken by his own screams. He reaches out for the glass of water he always keeps beside his bed but it is empty. He knows this is, without doubt, May's doing. He jumps out of bed and snaps on the light. The room is empty, but he looks under his bed just to make sure no one is lurking beneath. He has been on the alert ever since the night he woke to find Redcoat hovering over his bed. He has, since that day, harboured a special hatred for her. She reminds him of his own position in the mansion, though he is far better off.

The other secret he has kept hidden under his bed wriggles out into the light and begins to creep up his skin. He switches off the light and lies shuddering in his bed.

The secret pokes his ribs, forcing his mind to wander back to the night when he had similarly risen from his bed, awoken by an incredible thirst, and snapped on the light just to make sure no one was watching him. He had been jolted out of his skin as the light hit, not Redcoat, but this time a red-eyed May, seated starkly on the crumbling sofa they had stashed in his room.

'Kulay,' she had said in a stiff formal voice, quite unlike the tone in which she commanded him to slave about the mansion. There was a pause, during which Kulay stood undecided between the bed and the sofa.

'Kulay,' she said again, and this time forced herself to look directly into his eyes.

'May,' Kulay had recovered from the shock of seeing her seated in his room at that hour of the night and raised a threatening finger.

'Kulay,' she said again, and this time without pausing, added, 'how, how badly I wish you had never been born.'

Clemmie, awoken by Kulay's shouts, lies in the four-poster bed in May's bedroom thinking about the events of the day.

She had been the first to spy the sunken boat magically surfacing up from the lake. She had felt compelled to look at it and then beyond it to a spot behind the trees where her eyes had rested upon the sight of Kulay talking to a group of boys. Clemmie did not know who they were but sensed that they were up to no good. When she looked again the group had dissipated and Kulay was nowhere in sight.

Lying in the four-poster bed, Clemmie worries that Kulay has fallen into bad company for she knows that no good can ever come of the associations her wilful brother has ever forged.

Di lies wide awake watching Addy's eyes in soft focus as they caper to the haunts of Moon-Face and Pink-Whistle. The first light of day, creeping through the wakeful windows, tickles the sides of Addy's mouth full of words.

But Di, like her mother, is wordless with her own secrets. She is thinking of the stormy day when she had been led into the garage by an ill-meaning magic man.

Pages from *The Shillong Daily* were stuffed into the broken window pane to keep rain from entering the garage. The storm, however, did its best to wriggle through the little crevices whistling softly all the while.

She had felt the cold air prick her skin as her dress had been taken off.

Like a wrapper from a sweet.

In her To-Let bed she shivers weakly and pulls the mothballed quilt over her head. The world turns as dark as the first page of Addy's *Story of Creation* Book.

It is Very, Very Dark.

9. HOT AND CROSS

Unlike Ma, Addy has not given up the reading habit. But though she is ten, she cannot help delving now and then into the storybook for six-year-olds she has rediscovered in Kiyahoi's trunk. When she is sure no one is looking, Addy peeps into the book to find out how her friend Elizabeth Ann is getting along in her quirky quest for God's quintessence.

Unfortunately, sighs Addy, Elizabeth Ann's chances of meeting the Shillong man, who is a very important man and knows exactly how God began, are slim.

The man is Moishree Ditto's father. He is an important man and he knows exactly how God began.

'*She* not *he*,' Moishree screeches into my ear. 'Kali is our God.'

I'm hot and cross. It's going to be lunch-time but I won't eat. I sit waiting for the girls to go out to lunch. Clemmie goes out with Moishree because she has brought *rosogullas*.

'Kali Puja is coming! Kali Puja is coming!' Moishree does a queer little jig as she goes out.

I wait until it's quiet. Then I take out Moishree's box of coloured pencils and hide it in Clemmie's bag.

'Search your bags for Moishree's box,' Mrs Sen says, when Moishree complains about her missing box in the seventh period.

'Search your bag, Clemmie,' I say to Clemmie, who is standing up and staring into space.

'I didn't take it,' Clemmie says bringing out Moishree's box.

Thwack-thwack—Mrs Sen's ruler goes on Clemmie's fat little legs.

When she brings out her glasses to examine Clemmie's legs, they are red and swollen.

Clemmie begins to cry, but it's not enough and I am still hot and cross when it's time to go home.

'Clemmie,' I whisper through the door of May's kitchen so that Governor won't hear me.

Clemmie is washing red rice to cook in May's big black pot.

'Clemmie—I have an idea.'

'It's Sunday. I can't do bad things on Sunday,' Clemmie says when I tell her the idea.

She puts the pot on the fire and wipes her hands on her *jainkersha* like May does.

'Okay, I'll sing the song. You do the rest,' she says, unwilling to let down the friend who let her down because she was hot and cross.

We sneak up to Borthakur's gloomy quarters.

> *Brown-brown muddy-brown*
> *Put your panties up and down!*

Clemmie sings at the top of her voice while I dip my hands in the wet cool mud outside Borthakur's quarters and smear it on his freshly washed white sheets hanging in the sun.

'Haayeeeee!!!' Borthakur's son peers out of his gloomy window.

'You look like a frog,' Clemmie sticks her tongue out at him.

I try to tear the muddy sheets.

Then Borthakur jumps out of the door with a stick in his hand.

'*Brown-brown, muddy-brown,*' we sing, running full speed, and when we reach the mansion Clemmie screams:

'Governor, Governor save us from Borthakur.'

But I run right through the hedge when I hear Clemmie calling Governor and I sit there waiting for a long, long time.

I'm still hot and cross. Phoebe is flying kites with Kulay in the field. She flies kites and rides bicycles and she is big and happy. When she visits the lake, she jumps into the pretty red boat and tickles the water with her hands. Then she laughs some more and gives us little bits of *kwai* and I want to be like her because I don't want to be the skinny little girl frightened by Governor and I can't be anyone else.

'My father is Uncle Roy who sells sweets,' I tell them in school.

'Bring sweets for us.'

'Actually he's not my father, he's my uncle.'

'Who's your father?'

'Kilo Ram who sells meat.'

'Sweetmeat?'

But Clemmie asks me why my father doesn't come and asks if I'm hot and cross because of that.

'No.'

'If you write a letter to God you won't be hot and cross anymore.'

So I write one and Clemmie another and we bury it in the wet mud outside Borthakur's quarters, wondering why May says Borthakur's quarter and not Borthakur's half. Clemmie's letter to God asks him to forgive Kulay who has broken up Sissy Kay's tricycle and stolen pieces of tyres from the garage.

But the dogs dig up the letter in the night, fighting among themselves for buried bones. We hear the low growling sounds and the high-pitched howls as we sit huddled around the blue-flamed stove while Ma forgets to make dinner.

Kulay is making a small car. He is hoping it will turn out exactly like his mate Martin's. He is happy that he has befriended Martin, Terri, and Revise—the Union boys in St. James. They are from the localities that Shillong folk call the 'West.'

The wild, wild West.

Kulay has been mixing up with them for sometime now. He knows something is on. The Union has been planning a massive agitation. Something is surely afoot.

He has lingered behind them when they disappeared into the toilet to smoke. He has made personal visits to the stinking St. James toilet. He has gone out of the gates at lunch time and not bothered to go back. Secure in the knowledge that no one is going to do anything about it. No one can touch Martin or Terri or Revise... or Kulay. Or so he thinks.

Besides if anyone does anything about it, there is always the strike. St. James is famous for its strikes. If Martin, Terri and Revise were to spread the word, the whole school would unquestionably strike.

The Union has so far agitated peacefully for their demands. They have asked the government to withdraw the armed police force from the town, for they have been abusing their powers and terrorising the people. They have asked the government to make its papers publicly available so that no money goes where it mustn't.

The Union leaders have agreed to talk with the government about these demands but Kulay knows they are getting impatient as hunger spreads and jobs become scarce.

Kulay thinks of the corpulent and corrupt chief minister and his cabinet cronies in cahoots with the greedy *dkhars*. He feels his blood begin to stir at the unfairness of it all. He wishes for the strength to set things right. He wants to be as big and strong as Martin. He wants to have a car as big and strong as Martin's.

Martin had made a very elaborate car out of a broken tricycle and some good rubber tyres. It had a trailer attached to it. Martin was manning the steering wheel, which was nothing but a long wooden stick with a triangle on top where his hands rested.

He had gathered thirteen boys into it and raced down a hilltop at a speed that surpassed his own expectations. The *kali-het*, as the boys called it, picked up momentum and flew like the wind. As it circled the troubled town the thirteen boys banged on its side and cried: '*Dkhars* get out. *Dkhars* get out of town.'

Kulay loves the violence of Martin's contraption. He has found a large broken piece of glass to strengthen his kite strings. But when he spies Di plucking May's yellow mustard flowers, he pauses to peer at the girl.

Di imagines she is inside Addy's *Now We Are Six* book, plucking buttercups.

Close to her man,
Brown head, gold head
Lost among the buttercups.

'Look into my glass,' he says, imagining he is in his favourite Snow Queen story. 'Look into my glass,' he urges the girl, for he can see the hailstones described in the book and imagines each to be an exquisite flower. 'They are more interesting than real things *mein*! They are really perfect...'

Di looks into the glass and sees a thin brown face beside a boyish golden one that is blackened from burnt Mobil engine oil, but no flowers at all.

Kulay remembers his Union mates and hardens up. He pulls Di roughly towards the garage and pushes her beneath the dark Ambassador.

'Search for ball bearings,' he commands. 'Don't lift your dress... just search for ball bearings.'

He finds many and she finds none. The hard cement cracks her knee and when the blood appears thick and red, Kulay says, 'serves you right.'

'Suck it, suck it!' a dark patch like Sissy Kay whispers.

Kulay wriggles out from beneath the car and kicks him.

'I don't like Sissy Cake... I like the harder stuff...'

Two sisters and two first cousins sit in a large smoky kitchen and engage in a discussion about what is going to happen to Kulay and whether Curiosity-the-cat can possibly be a Cheshire Cat.

Clemmie has seen two policemen outside the mansion gate and worries that they might be looking for Kulay.

'Maybe they know he's keeping bad company,' she says fearfully, but Phoebe ignores her and begins to stroke the cat.

'Cheshire Puss,' Phoebe calls. 'Cheshire Puss, will I turn into a spinster of Shillong one day?'

'What's that, Phoebe?'

'Spinster means to live alone.'

'Alone?'

'May is going to be a spinster.' Clemmie is making little balls out of the dough that Phoebe has kneaded.

'Don't tell lies, Mujupeas.'

'Yes, it's true. She's going to live alone in her house on the hill... Gujupeas.'

Kulay's *kali-het* is a failure. It runs a little way and then stops lethargically. Kulay gets off angrily to see what the matter is. He kicks at it fiercely.

Someone is watching him. Someone looks at the *kali-het* and then at its driver.

A policeman.

The boy's heart begins to pound. Does this man know he has been mixing up with the Union boys who are wanted for disturbing the peace? Slowly, lovingly almost, he pushes the *kali-het* back up the slope.

'We have a new girl called Kelsang.' Mrs Sen scratches her bum.

From the front of the class Clemmie turns to check if I noticed. I nod to Clemmie and she covers her mouth in silent laughter.

The new girl is wearing a tan coloured dress. She has no uniform yet.

Mrs Sen makes her sit next to Clemmie. Clemmie is happy to be with Kelsang because she smiles shyly and forgets to look at me.

At lunch-time everyone gathers around Kelsang.

'You're Naga or Mizo?' Moishree asks her.

'No.'

'But you have chinky eyes.'

'I'm Tibetan,' Kelsang says and runs towards the Monkey Jump.

We follow her screaming, because she has climbed to the top and is hanging upside down.

May stands in the garden near the swing, cutting the green chillies she had planted in the summer.

'It's my birthday tomorrow,' Clemmie swings gaily.

'The winds have arrived,' May says, looking at the sky.

There are many coloured kites in the sky.

Kulay goes around the mansion with a mad look in his eyes. He is looking for fused bulbs. He wants to crush them into glass to make 'mynja'—a special liquid to strengthen his kite strings.

'Allied-checkpoint-Charlie-calling-Allied-checkpoint-Johnny,' Kulay chants, as he goes about in circles.

Soon he is hard at work on the lawn. He dips a thick rag into a tin of dirty yellow mynja and runs it down the length of kite-string tied from one tree to another one far away.

'Fetch the thin bamboo sticks,' Kulay commands, forgetting to add 'Skinny Devil' because he is hard at work.

I gather the thin bamboo sticks and hand them to Kulay.

'Thanks,' Kulay almost smiles because his *mynja* is thick and strong. Soon he will be soaring in the sky with the purple kite that lies in the grass wagging its frilly white tail.

Governor drives up through the gate in the Ambassador, which is now painted like a taxi. Redcoat is sitting at the back. The car is loaded with groceries.

'Look May, look,' Clemmie sings, swinging still higher.

'Tell that man I'm going to live in my new house and never coming back,' May threatens. 'Go Clemmie, go. Go and tell that man.'

Clemmie grabs my hand. We run in the wind behind Governor's taxi.

'May said she's going away.'

'Tell her I've got other women,' Governor whispers. He puts his hand on Redcoat's back as he helps her unload the groceries. Clemmie searches his pocket for sweets.

'He said he's got other women.' We are breathless by now as we run back and forth.

May grabs Clemmie by the shoulder.

'I'll kill you, Governor. I'll kill you.' May grinds her teeth, marching past Governor and dragging Clemmie.

Addy is looking important again. We are trying to decide what we'll give Clemmie on her birthday.

'Decide. Decide.' I can't wait to go to Clemmie's house and give her the present.

'Let's make a list.' Addy fetches her notebook and pencil. 'Let's make a list and then select the best one from it.'

We draw the curtains on the window that looks out on to Clemmie's house.

'Climb inside the quilt,' Ma says disconsolately.

I climb under it but something touches my back.

'Don't be silly,' Addy snorts, concentrating on her List of Possible Presents for Clemmie.

'Addy there's someone's hand behind me.'

'It's an imaginary hand,' Addy says, pushing up her glasses. She tries to scratch it out of my back until it stings.

The hand drums its fingers harder.

Addy gets her wooden ruler from her school bag and scratches my back with it.

'Has it gone?'

I don't tell Addy that its Governor's hand dancing on my back and it will never go.

Kulay opens the door when we ring the bell on Clemmie's birthday.

'Take off your *topias*, Green Devils,' Kulay tries to snatch off our green woollen caps.

'Utopia?' Addy suppresses an erudite burp.

'What have you Green Devils brought with you... checkpoint Charlie?'

'We'll give it to Clemmie,' Addy says, taking off her cap.

'You take off your *topia* too.'

I take off my green cap too and we hold our caps in our hands and fiddle with them.

Kulay grabs our present and tears it open.

'That's for moi kite.' He stuffs the wrapping paper in his pocket. 'Never give me a book for my birthday.'

'Why?' Addy asks bravely.

'Because I'll tear it up. That's why—the sky is so high—you'll marry in July... *dkhars*.'

'Why do you call us *dkhar*?' Addy is brave and angry.

'Because you are.'

'We're not. We're Indian.'

'Indians get out,' Kulay tries to bully us but Clemmie appears in her new birthday dress, which is orange and has permanent pleats. Clemmie takes the book from Kulay.

'Enter,' Kulay opens the door for us. 'Enter and be entertained.'

May has arranged the tall chairs in the sitting room. The piano is covered with birthday cards for Clemmie and there is a big balloon on the ceiling. Addy climbs onto the tall chairs and swings her legs.

'Ha! Ha!' Governor enters holding a huge needle in his hand. I hide behind Addy.

Clemmie wipes Governor's kiss fiercely from her cheek.

Governor bursts the huge balloon. Sweets go shattering in all directions.

'We're going to get high tea,' Clemmie scrambles for the sweets and gets the most.

May enters through the bead curtains holding a plate of cake high above her head. She gives us tiny pieces. Sissy Kay hides his piece in his hanky.

'To eat later.'

'I don't want high tea, May,' Kulay is wrapping his kite string around a tin box. 'May, I don't want high tea—I want the harder stuff.'

'Don't talk like THAT man,' May says pointing at Governor.

Governor is stuffing a piece of cake into his mouth but he gets up when May points at him.

'Teach them young, May,' he says roaring through the bead curtains.

May marches out behind Governor.

'I'm a victim of your vices,' May screams.

'Go and play,' Governor tells us. 'Don't listen to grown-ups. Go and play.'

'My parents break windows when they fight,' Kelsang says as we mill around her at lunch time. 'What about yours?'

10. FESTIVAL OF FIGHTS

'Governor will have to pay me the rent if he lives in the mansion because it's my house... officially,' May spits *kwai* juice into the hedge viciously.

Ma and May are having a chat over the hedge.

'Are you really going?' Ma asks touching May's arm. 'Don't go.'

Ma invites May for a cup of tea. She sits uncomfortably in the cramped kitchen and drinks only half the tea.

'I have another house now.' May puts on her time-for-the-Witch expression. 'I must make use of it.' She gets up and moves into the inner room inspecting the walls.

'Why don't you whitewash the house?' she asks suddenly.

'I can't afford it.'

'I'll send that man to do it.'

'Just as well that the house gets a whitewash before Diwali,' Ma thinks sullenly.

May makes as if to leave but hesitates at the threshold.

'Do you know Benjamin Budoor?' she asks abruptly.

'No,' Ma says. 'I don't know that many people.'

'Hurry! I want to see the naked woman, girls...'

Sissy Kay comes running out with a spoon in his mouth. His tie is undone and his bag is falling off his shoulder. He trips on his untied shoelaces.

'And you'll stay in class Eight next year too!' May scolds Sissy Kay because we are all late for school.

'But we'll go to class Five,' Clemmie pokes a finger inside her red gum boots in case the toad that startled her yesterday is still hiding there.

'Helter-skelter,' Sissy Kay lifts up Clemmie's skirt as she bends down.

'Grow up, Sissy Kay,' Clemmie marches off without an umbrella.

'The early worm catches the bird,' Sissy Kay winks at me, and races ahead in the rain.

A big crowd of schoolboys has gathered around the naked woman.

The woman gathers rainwater in a brass pot and pours it over herself.

The school boys whistle and hoot.

Addy, Clemmie and I look away.

In school, Moishree Ditto is uncontrollably excited at the approaching festival of lights. Her father, however, is circumspect for he knows that trouble often comes along with any festival of the *dkhars*.

Mr Ditto comes to fetch Moishree Ditto from school, panicking. He enters the classroom long before the bell sounds and, stumbling on the row of green and blue chairs, announces to Mrs. Sen that the shops are shutting down.

'Mr Ditto, you are getting panicky,' Mrs Sen tries to prevent Moishree Ditto's father from entering the class with the ruler that had thwacked Clemmie's fat little legs.

'There's trouble in TOWN! Shops are shutting DOWN.' Moishree begins to screech as she overhears her father arguing with Mrs Sen.

'Your father looks like a monkey,' Kelsang marches up to Moishree. 'Your father looks just like a monkey.'

Moishree stops screeching. She picks up her bag and walks out quietly with Mr Ditto who walks panicking all the way home.

'I think she's a bride,' Addy says adjusting her spectacles and looking at the idol of a woman with many hands.

'She is a bride,' Addy says, peering at the street through a To-Let window. The bride is travelling in a rickety truck called Public Carrier. Public Carrier is wearing golden streamers on its forehead. The men in the truck dance about the bride as they give her an airing. But they will drown her at the end of the festivities in October.

Ma sees this and rushes into the kitchen. She is silent, for she knows that the woman is no bride but a goddess. But then, even goddesses are abandoned she thinks disconsolately. Perhaps that's why he had left her. Because she had tried to love him unconditionally, as a goddess might love her worshippers. She wonders if she would have been better off, had she been more like May. Was May happy? Why did she want to know about Benjamin Budoor? Who was Benjamin Budoor anyway?

She has not thought of any other man herself, for she had buried her roots in him. He was her promised land. She had buried her secrets in this land. The land was fertile to her. It had many dreams. She liked to snuggle inside the pits of its arms, which were mystery caves, dark and sombre. She had often traced routes along its veins with the forbidden tip of her forefinger. She had many plans to travel over this land and to explore. She had learnt to tolerate its smells and wait. She knew when to get lost in it, when to divide it against itself, when to love it and when to hate. She knew of its floods and its flowers. But it had turned against her and left her alone.

> *I will not*
> *Hold you*
> *Kiss you*
> *Sleep with you*
> *If that's ok then you can stay.*

But the shameless woman had wanted just that.

To be held, kissed, slept with.

Ma tears down the furnishings of the To-Let House and places them on the grass in preparation for Governor's whitewashing.

'This is no time to be lying in bed,' she says, spanking Di who is dreaming.

Di is dreaming of Phoebe.

Phoebe, in Di's dream, is learning how to drive Governor's great black car. Di watches Phoebe in the rear view mirror. Phoebe is smiling in proud concentration as she drives slowly past Kulay's school.

It is 5 a.m. when Ma ruins her dream.

The Diwali spirit is in the air. The sky has a comely clarity in the day but the evenings are austere and grey. Winter is round the bend. The end of another year is only two months away.

Ma stuffs all the quilts in a mammoth gunny sack and drags it outside.

When Addy opens the sack to give the quilts an airing, Curiosity-the-cat emerges from it yawning insolently.

'How are you getting on?' she appears to ask Addy, who waits for the cat's ears to appear before she answers.

Poor Addy. She does often confuse fact with fiction.

'How do you like May?' asks Curiosity-the-cat in a low voice.

'Not too much,' says Addy. 'She's so remarkably...'

Curiosity-the-cat sniffs at this and that, then raising her head remarks, 'May is rather dismal these days.'

Addy knows this is because May does not really want to leave the mansion. When she turns around to address the cat, she has disappeared and, much to Addy's disappointment, has taken her grin with her.

Pickpocketing is on the rise in Shillong especially in the buses. Ma is busy making an inventory of the things she has lost.

Governor arrives, swishing his whitewash tins. He stands for a while surveying the belongings of the To-Let House which appear to be growing out of the grass.

'Mauve or Strawberry or Surf Blue or Aquamarine?' he asks Ma, bowing with each colour of distemper he offers.

'Whitewash,' says Ma politely.

'Primrose or Merrie Pink or Bathstone or Barley?' he insists and this time he is decidedly singing.

'Whitewash,' says Ma blushing. She is beginning to suspect that the profusion of colours has something to do with the nature of her eyes.

Having spoken so little to so few up till now, Governor's presence does curious things to her. She blushes and she flaps, exclaiming and expressing, but never once questioning him about the day of the storm.

But even Governor cannot distract her from her memories and she returns to them remembering how she had tried to win him back after she found him drifting away from her. She had hoped to rekindle his love for her. She had promised him insanely to do as he wished, submitting herself to the joy of servitude.

'You may do as you like.'

He had convinced himself he was not looking for redemption—only for an unfettered life.

But she looked down and said, 'I will do as you ask.'

He lit a cigarette in the dank darkness and sucked it deeply without any pleasure.

His hand to her face. His unhappy finger twirling her hair. The throwing to the floor, the snarling and crying, the roaring and reproach... that was for later. The silver-tongued silence suspended between them is what she remembers.

He put his cigarette to her lips. He made a mistress out of her. He forbade her to dictate the terms of his life.

I am cruel, cruel, cruel, he cried out in his weakness.

'Sahib, Biwi aur Gulam,' booms Governor startling her out of her reverie.

He begins to whistle a tune from the Hindi film of that name.

She exclaims ecstatically at the melodious whistling tune, while he swishes his great big brush up and down the faded walls.

'How do you know these tunes?'

Her voice almost breaks at 'tunes' for she has never spoken this much or with such excitement in a long, long while.

'I love Hindi movies,' Governor says and whistles the tunes that surprise Ma.

Ma makes Governor a cup of tea on the kitchen stove, which stands under the spindly orange trees. He gulps it down and asks for more.

'Wipe the floor,' she says. 'Di, take a rag and wipe the whitewash patches from the floor.'

She hands Governor a second cup of tea and says, 'Wipe Uncle's boots too—they're full of whitewash.'

'You can call me Governor, Madam,' Governor laughs.

'Is that really your name?'

'People all over the world have strange names. But I don't.'

Governor mixes in the tin with a stick and works silently for a while.

He turns to Ma suddenly.

'My wife is a sarcastic woman. And what's more she's going to buy a television. She's going to buy a television from the rent that I pay her...,' he roars drunkenly. 'She's a sarcastic woman.'

Ma smiles politely.

I bend my head and try to work at Governor's boots.

They turn into a bright night sky with a thousand whitewashed moons, which grin at me as if they know it all.

When the festival of lights comes, everything is dark in the To-Let House.

The shops below are teeming with fireworks but Ma knows she cannot touch a thing. 'If I buy a few packets of crackers for my children I am already half-broke.' For the first time since she has moved into the To-Let House, Ma is animated.

She glances wistfully at her rich neighbours. Governor has bought sparklers and crackers wholesale. Clemmie has been bursting crackers non-stop for the last eight days.

Di is still shining the boot that Governor has left behind. The light emanating from the moon spies Di busy at the boots as it filters through the laces. She wonders what her own father does for his boots and shoes since he lives at the bottom of the dark blue sea.

'Boots and shoes under the sea,' says Addy in the voice of her favourite Griffin from *Alice in Wonderland*, 'are done with whiting.'

'And what are they made of?' Di asks with deepening curiosity for she knows that an average pair of men's shoes costs a lot of money.

Governor had told her this on their excursions to the garage. He had held the frightened mite by her skinny shoulders and asked her to tell him why, when he went to the Shillong Secretariat,

The Ministaars of the State
They arrived so late?

When Di failed to answer his question, he threatened to lift up her dress with the tip of his boots, and informed her that they were a costly pair indeed, unlike her hard wooden clogs that made her little feet awfully sore and red. His boots had been bought in a local Chinese shop and in China there were a great many wonderful things.

Di, having heard the story of Governor's boots, had developed a peculiar affinity for the strange things.

'What are they made of?' Di repeats for she is bursting with curiosity.

'Soles and eels of course,' snorts Addy, impatient with her slow sister for she has read her *Alice in Wonderland* seven times.

May comes around with a candle to see what the To-Let family is doing for the night since they are still living out on the grass. Two green stars appear by the stove where Curiosity-the-cat is warming herself.

'Come and sleep in my house,' says May to the dreaming sisters and they follow her obediently, leaving Ma to guard the whitewashed house for she dare not go.

As they make their way to the mansion, the two girls see rockets streaming across the sky and hear chocolate bombs being let off on the street. The neighbourhood boys are bursting crackers near old women, making them jump.

Kulay stands at the mansion wall watching them coldly. He is waiting for the patriots—Martin, Terri and Revise. They are against the *dkhar* festival and will try to put an end to it. Such acts are frowned upon by the Union, but the boys indulge in them anyway. It gives them a high to fearlessly face up to the *dkhars* and ask them to either leave or, as Terri likes to put it, 'face the music.'

Addy is worried that Ma will be visited in the night. Perhaps by the patriots or by passers-by. They might peer into the To-Let House saying:

> A little clay hut
> With windows shut.
> Yoo-hoo! Anyone inside?

What is Ma doing, she wonders. Little does she know that the woman, making hay while the girls are away, has put on her wedding sari and the gaudy tinsel trinkets they have never seen. She is standing on the street hoping against hope that he, seeing her thus dressed, will feel a rekindling of the great passion he once had for her.

Is that him? She squints. Is that walking contradiction him?

Oh where is he? Where, she wonders, is the crusader who wanted to change the world? Where is the man who had sworn to let his hair grey with hers? Where is the father of the dust-laden children?

'There he is,' she cries into the emptiness. 'There he is, hiding from his deeds.'

She stands there, envying him his peace for he must indeed be very peaceful now having driven her stark, raving mad.

The mansion looks very different in the dark. Di, who is trembling in her pants, thinks that it resembles a 'hut on hen's feet with one lighted window, which keeps turning round and round.'

It is the effect of May's hearth, and under its kind warmth, Di falls to dreaming a great many troubled dreams.

She sees May pick up her olive-coloured knitting and is sure this is Baba-Yaga's hut where the real Witch sits spinning her tow. Baba-Yaga will soon hand her the spindle and go out. As the little girl sits there spinning, a mouse runs out from under the stove and says to her:

'Lassie, lassie, give me some porridge and I will tell you something.'

The little girl gives it some porridge, and the mouse says, 'Baba-Yaga has gone to make a fire in the bath-house. She will steam you and wash you, roast you in the oven and eat you up, and then take a ride on your bones.'

Di knows this is not true for despite her sorcery it is none other than May who has given them shelter for the night. She gives the mouse a little more porridge for she knows it has true things to tell her.

When the mouse whispers the true things in her ear the little girl begins crying and trembling with fear.

Di wakes up startled and runs outside to join Addy who is wide awake watching Clemmie burst her mountain of crackers while Governor dances to their tune.

Suddenly, the mansion is alight and ablaze. Governor is in very high spirits as he dances around Clemmie's lighted fountains. He rushes to the wall that looks out onto the crackling streets and bursting into eloquence, magnificently proclaims: 'On this one day darkness does not have any shelter in the darkest caves or even in the eyes of the blindest man.'

At this, several stones are hurled at the roof of the mansion. Martin, Terri, Revise and Kulay – the straggly band of patriots – attack, cursing Governor for the ugly Hindi film songs which are emanating from the turquoise coloured shops where the shopkeepers are playing their radio.

The two sides of the road are festooned with flowers of light.

'Almighty Lord was in Shillong when he said, 'let there be light',' says one fanatic who has strayed through the gate and into the mansion compound in a rush of misplaced religious fervour. 'Diwali goes but the light remains. It is a blissful gift to us.'

'And the Almighty Father was right when he saw the light was good. And we should wipe our faces with our two palms and say Amen,' says Governor, and with that he gives the man a resounding kick and sends him flying through the gate at which the latter stands trying to urinate, until Governor drags his paint and brush to that very spot and paints the words:

Pissing Is Prohibited

The three little girls forget the sparklers in their hands as they watch these activities in utter merriment.

By the time Addy, Di and Clemmie are herded indoors, their ears are smoky with sleep.

But Governor steers them into the kitchen for he still has a great many stories to tell. Stories of the earthquake in which his ancestors perished, and tales of the blood-hungry demons which he spices up for the merriment of Permanent Pleats and her skinny friends.

Clemmie has turned into Permanent Pleats since the day of her birthday when she acquired two little permanently pleated dresses. She wears this attire untiringly, crosses her chubby legs and listens with rapt astonishment when Governor, preceded by his black liquor breath, transforms himself into a blood-hungry demon.

He tears out his arms from his sordid shawl, trying to exhibit how the earthquake hit his forefathers in the most unpremeditated of ways. In a terrible embrace, it had wrung out all human habitation.

Clang!
Clang!
Clang!

Governor throws May's kettles and pans about as he tries to demonstrate his seismic story. The tale possesses him and he goes to great lengths to describe the earth's fury, for he knows better than most men the evils it harbours in its breast and how ugly it can choose to be.

As hillsides upturn and forests dissolve into sand, Governor grows in size until he towers over the merry miniatures like a great giant of stone that no earthquake can ever shake.

Soon, very soon, he will begin to take great sniffs and turn his head this way and that. 'I can smell fresh meat,' he will roar, and and the children will, referring to the larder, timidly answer 'that must be the pig inside Tom Dooley which May is keeping for you.' Ignoring this, the giant will bellow, 'I can smell fresh cuts...' And this time he will take one big stride and moving towards the skinniest mite will say: 'Oh! Miserable children, here is meat enough for my three forefathers who will eat with me in a day or three. Do you think you can suck before I do?' And with that he will lift skinny Di high into the air and say, 'the fatter you get, the better you will be for feasting.'

Di wishes at this point that she could turn into Permanent Pleats for surely the giant will not harm the legs that are covered in a permanently pleated dress. And as his thick fingers fumble in the darkness of the garage, and press heavily into the permanent pleats he might grunt: 'Permanent Pleats! Permanent Pleats! These must be the wrong legs,' and then he might lurch over to other softer shapes.

So weary are the girls by the time Governor's stories end that they fall upon May's four-poster bed and are soon in another country.

They huddle together on the ominous bed while May's Baba-Yaga fire chuckles before them. Though three heads disappear under the covers, Di lies there darkly, listening to May revise the adult alphabet for she claims that such a thing exists and is to be found in the Book of Books.

Di hears the floorboards creak as Governor enters the room and holds her breath as he rummages under the bed to find his seven-league boots.

He is ready to travel over great heights and drunken distances. Soon the sound of quarrelling voices reaches her sleepy ears for the man and his wife have raised their voices as they argue about this and that.

Unknown to them, Di hears everything they say. She grows frightened at the thought of what she has learnt. She fervently wishes it is not true.

She wonders where Kulay has gone. She finds the bully's absence curious for she has grown used to watching him watch her. How achingly she wishes to leap out of the interminable bed and rush to the kitchen to find out the veracity of things being revealed in that corner.

The distant fire is sizzling with the wrath that the man and his wife spew at each other. A clandestine cat comes skulking out from the kitchen. Curiosity-the-cat leaps onto the bed and settles down. The cat snores stealthily as she weighs down heavily on Di's sore red feet.

The girl knows it is now impossible to run to the kitchen and discover that May and Governor are only a pack of cards after all and she needn't be afraid of them.

Addy is dreaming of the things that start with 'M' when May's footsteps sound in the bedroom and she snaps on the light.

'I'm going to teach you a song,' May pulls the quilt roughly from our sleeping heads.

'No,' sleepy Clemmie says angrily, sniffing the whisky fumes on May's breath and grinding her teeth.

She wishes May will turn into an ant so that she can crush the life out of her.

> How'd you do my partner?
> How'd you do to-day?
> Shall we da-ance to-gether
> I shall show you the way.

Curiosity-the-cat wakes up with a grunt. May puts her mouth near Clemmie and sings into her ears.

'Get out, bitch...,' Governor shrieks her into silence. May drags us shivering into the cold open lawn.

'Moonlight heals a hurting heart,' May says to the three shuddering girls settling on the grass.

She had visited Benjamin's villa the previous day. When, through his window, he saw her approaching, he had pretended to be hard at thought.

Hesitatingly, she asked him if she was disturbing him and politely he answered no. After the discussion about Sissy Kay was over, she had been inclined to stay a while but the man had not been forthcoming. It was increasingly hard to keep the conversation going after that.

May was close to tears by the time she left, for she knew how hard it was, as one got older, to make the friendships one so effortlessly made in one's youth.

She had wanted to leave the mansion and start again. But she wanted to start again with Benjamin. Now that he had not been forthcoming, her resolve to leave weakened a little. She knew she couldn't leave until she had him.

It is only at dawn that the children are allowed to return to their warm bed and the mansion falls asleep. They trundle inside the quilt like three pieces of ice and bit by bit begin to melt back into sleep.

11. UNIONS

Four heads stick out from the barred, unpainted window of the To-Let House one rainy day as Ma rushes out to fetch her lemons before the rain ruins them.

And three tongues tingle while Addy makes up jingles.

The tongues of Kulay, Clemmie and Di.

'What are those things your Ma is carrying?'

'What things?'

'Those *alllh-loooh* type of things.'

'Lemons.'

'What are you?'

'Hindu.'

'What do you do?'

'We put dots on our head.'

'That dot. That "on-the-dot" dot?'

'No.'

'What is your Ma making?'

'*Pakoras.*'

'Give us some. Give us some fuckoras.'

Ma brushes the raindrops from her hair slowly. Perhaps she should stop expecting a letter to arrive. Perhaps she should start occupying more of her own present and less of his absence.

She is startled out of her melancholic reverie by the sound of Kulay's footsteps as he creeps up behind her with cupped hands, burning in shame to be asking a *dkhar*, yet craving to eat some fuckoras.

Ma pours a couple of pakoras into his hands. Kulay thinks guiltily of Clemmie who has been dragged away by May to attend Sunday school.

A small pakora goes rolling out of his hands and after a short distance comes to a standstill. He pops one reluctantly into his mouth, hoping it will melt without him having to chew. After he has eaten he rubs his hands and folds them. He sits silently looking out onto the street with large troubled eyes.

From the kitchen, Ma hears Kiyahoi's trunk creaking as Kulay lifts its heavy lid to find the story of the Snow Queen and read it for the hundredth time.

He shrugs up his shoulders until his neck disappears and crosses his legs. He narrows his eyes and scans the book, enlarging them again and blinking slowly. He smirks at a fly trying to tickle the corners of his mouth. He blinks again. Before his eyes, he can see a small hailstone grow and grow until it takes the shape of a woman dressed in the finest white veil that seems to be made of millions of shiny starry flakes. 'She is extremely beautiful and grand but she is made of ice, glittering, dazzling ice, yet she is alive. Her eyes shine like two bright stars but there is no peace in them. She nods towards the window and beckons with her hands.'

A big swallow flies past the window.

At last, Kulay thinks, at long, long last, I know it exists—a world illuminated by strong Northern Lights. An incredibly large, fearfully empty, icy cold and dazzlingly white world.

He gets up abruptly feeling ashamed of himself. What if Martin, Terri and Revise come to know of his fantasies? What if they smell the fuckoras on his breath?

Ma is peeping into her black pots. Perhaps she will turn around and, like the Snow Queen, say, 'I'm off to warmer countries...' But she just stands up and drags a large black cloth to cover the windows for the sight of the street without a hint of him is beginning to gnaw her.

Kulay digs his heels into the ground with rage.

He walks in the wet lawn scratching a rash and itching for a kite.

It is getting towards evening and a great many upheavals have taken place in the life of the mansion family.

But for now Kulay is wearing Los Angeles on his dirty denim baseball cap. His waterproof drainpipe pants have a thick stripe of happy yellow sun dribbling all the way down from his hips to his ankles.

Curiosity-the-cat zigzags sulkily across his path. He kicks her hard. She flies into the air at an angle, her wet fur standing on edge.

The field is too slushy to play football though Kulay is wearing his football boots. The cheap, reconditioned ones to which he has added spikes.

He kicks hard in the grass. He leans on the high stone wall that runs round the mansion and watches the street.

He scratches madly at his rash. He loves it when it starts to itch under his skin. It fills his head with a burning desire for a single spectacular something he cannot name.

His stony eyes glint with deep longings.

But his tongue is tingling.

Fuck the fuckoras.

F-U-C-K. He writes with his finger on the windscreen of the Aston Martin, rearranging the settled dust.

The St. James jerks, driven indoors by the rain, will be out soon. He returns to the stone wall and watches out for them. Martin, Terri, and Revise are out first.

Three multi-coloured dots move in an uncertain swagger across the slushy football field.

When the troublesome trio enters the wrought iron gate of the mansion, they notice a woman in a deep red sari exiting it.

Redcoat.

Martin motions to Kulay to follow suit and the foursome proceed behind her as she makes her way to the last kiosk in the shady row of shops running all along the foot of the mansion.

Unlike its counterparts, Solomon's Mines, the kiosk Redcoat is heading towards, is a sore black thumb sticking out from the uniform turquoise coloured sea of petty shops rented out to the Bihari Brothers, as Kulay calls them. Suresh, Dinesh and their uncle, Munchy Rai, are buried deep inside the ration shop conferring about May's hike in the rent.

Mr Gooptu, the Bengali who owns the sweet shop, stands at the threshold and bows ineffectively at the sight of the troublesome trio and the sinister straggler following behind.

He knows where the team is headed. He knows he must bow when they pass. He is burdened by the knowledge that the boys could bully him; could bulldoze him out of the sweet shop with a sour slap. Mr Gooptu brings his hand to his face remembering the hard slap he once received from a Khasi youth whom he had tried to stop from running away with a jar of unpaid-for sweets.

He hastily picks up a newspaper to hide his face from the boys.

But Redcoat, nearing Solomon's Mines, snatches Mr Gooptu's defence, deeming it necessary for her own survival against the advancing army.

'A black magic woman,' Terri mutters, keeping a safe distance from her hurrying back.

Kulay, trailing behind the trio, takes in, with rising anger, the big red *bindi*, the bigger nose ring and the biggest eyes he has ever seen. He notes with disgust, the melanin patches falling out of Redcoat's face and stops at a puddle to examine his own unblemished skin, unscarred by either patches or pimples.

He struggles to catch up with the trio who is stalking ahead.

'They are ignoring me now but I'll show them...' he thinks, resolving to drink some *jeera pani* at Solomon's Mines to cure his tingling tongue.

When they arrive, Borthakur, their procurer of *cannabis indica*, is standing outside the shady shop pulling hard on a chillum, bringing up the flames.

Martin, Terri and Revise stand conferring in a corner.

Their voices reach Kulay on a slow swaying wave.

'You want to join the Union? They're taking new members today.'

'For what?' Kulay feigns an indifference he does not actually feel.

'What not.'

He feels the tug of a dazzlingly white world that the word 'union' evokes.

'Is it possible?' he asks the boys, quaking faintly.

'In the Union,' they say enigmatically, 'all things are possible.'

Yes. Yes. Yes. He wants to join the Union. He wants only white skin and red blood and pure shit.

The boy knows he should return home but his feet are frozen into the ground.

He knows he will never be forgiven, but his heart has turned to stone. He does not once look back over his shoulder to see the mansion, though he feels the eyes of the ghostly manor boring into the small of his neck. Still he has never wanted that home and, he thinks bitterly, it has never wanted him. All he wants now is to feel at home in the dazzlingly white world he imagines opening before him.

Redcoat peers out of the shop's single window and spits at the curious colour of Kulay's wants..

'*Naam Salty aur kaam namak harami,*' swears Munchy Rai, referring to May by her Christian name as he emerges from his shop half an hour later. He stops swearing when he sees Kulay standing at the threshold of Solomon's Mines sucking a Phantom candy cigarette. Kulay is waiting for his feet to become light enough for him to run away with Martin, Terri and Revise into the Motinagar forests, high up on the hill beyond the mosque.

Munchy Rai tentatively hitches up his white dhoti, revealing his hairy legs. He is wearing dark green socks and black rexene shoes.

'Ai Munchy Rai...*ghar jao mein,*' Kulay hisses through his bright red mouth where the Phantom fire has left its colour.

Ignoring him, Munchy Rai looks up at Clemmie who is leaning from the stone wall that runs around the mansion. She is holding two tiny teacups to her chest in mock breast imitation.

'*Arre! Clemmie toh mahila ho gayee...*' Munchy Rai grinds his *khaini* energetically.

Kulay comes up behind Munchy Rai and spits in his face just as he is about to bring the *khaini* to his mouth.

'*Saala Kutta...*' Munchy Rai yells.

Smelling trouble, the petty traders begin to draw the shutters of their shop.

But Kulay is already racing across the street.

Clemmie watches him diminishing into a dot as he splashes through the wet field and runs past the fire brigade building, past the mosque and up onto the steep climb leading to the Motinagar forests. He sees Lou Majaw and the Blood & Thunder blokes rehearsing for their upcoming concert outdoors.

'Lou! Lou! Teach me Kung Fu,' he yells running past.

'Bloody hell,' Lou calls out looking like a summit in his chopped jeans and his long windy hair. 'Bloody hell.'

And then he reaches the forest.

A cold wave of water explodes into his face.

Martin, Terri and Revise have plunged into the vast water reservoirs.

Kulay spies an easy prey in the pines and aims his catapult at it. He notices that the snares for wild hen are already in place. He wants to see a leopard. He has heard the jackals in the dead of the night when May's drunken sobs subside and dread grips his heart.

The bird whizzes past and the stone bullet falls to the ground with a thud. He feels an incredible lightness rustling through his entire being.

He ignores the hooters in the water and walks towards the pine trees. He tears out a tin cone attached to the pine tree. It is full of resin which the villagers will later turn into turpentine. He goes on a rampage tearing out as many tin cones as he can gather from each bleeding tree. He will set them on fire tonight, for tonight he will be free.

This Little Pig stayed at home...

Sissy Kay is warming himself before May's fireplace the night that Kulay joins the Union. He is feeling horribly cosy and horribly holier-than-thou for Clemmie has told him that she's seen Kulay disappearing into the forests and has expressed her doubts about his return.

Sissy Kay is going to tell May, just you wait and see. In her merciful meanness, May would certainly lend her ears to the tall little tattle-tit for she does have a score or two to settle with her stony son.

Besides she must lend her ear to the poor little orphan boy, for didn't she have a wicked little thought in her head on the day of the doomed jeep?

And didn't Reverend OntheWay give her a knowing nod this rainy Sunday morning when she arrived in church, in the palest of pink *jainsems* and the reddest of red gum boots, dragging a wet little shrivelled up Clemmie to attend Sunday school?

> *Good Girls go to Heaven*
> *Bad Boys go to Hell-o!*

Sissy Kay informs his gold-laden aunt. He sticks little snot balls under his soft leather boots, which May has bought him to appease the spirits of Margaret M and Damien D, which she fears hovering, right above the haughty red roof that protects her head.

The resin tins burn big and bright. Kulay watches coldly.

That night in the To-Let House, Ma has dipped her hands inside the trunk again when she hears a rat-a-tat-tat on the door. She goes to the window and sees Borthakur peering inside holding a hose in his hand.

He has come to douse the fire burning within her, he says, when she opens the door. 'Perhaps he is drunk,' she thinks but she is not afraid.

It is dark but she does not turn on the lights for fear of waking Addy and Di. Instead, she lights the kerosene lamp and leads him towards the orange trees.

They sit in silence.

The smell of kerosene from the lamp mingles with the sound of crickets.

Borthakur picks up a splinter from the ground and pokes his teeth. Has she heard of the Assamiya *bhoot*, he asks.

No.

The worst ones to catch you are the Nepali ghosts, he says.

She looks at him unalarmed.

'Now I confirm that he is still in Shillong,' he chuckles through his rotting teeth.

'Are you sure?' Her knees tremble.

He laughs inexplicably.

The same feeling of ludicrous grief that had filled her when she first met Borthakur rushes through her again.

She inhales the opiate air deeply. Borthakur sucks strongly on his *beedi*. He twirls a little ball of leaves between his forefinger and thumb, humming softly as she leaves him wordlessly and moves into the house.

Perhaps she would have been happier if he had left the town. But he was in this very place. Perhaps he had started a new life. How had he forgotten her so quickly?

She cowers on the floor of the dark To-Let House shaken by what Borthakur has told her. She hears things whispering through the books in Kiyahoi's trunk. But she no longer feels compelled by their magic.

He had obliterated her from memory. But when he had finally set her free, she wanted more than anything else to return to him.

Had he turned into a hermit or a messiah? Had he returned to the world, married again, carried on as if nothing had changed?

The night had no answers. The only thing it could tell her was that he had changed sides.

She returns into the cold carrying an armful of books. Borthakur stands up at the sight of this woman threatening to collapse under the weight of the books or perhaps the weight of her grief.

She smashes the kerosene lamp on the books and, snatching his beedi, lights up the pile. Borthakur shakes his head from side to side but does not douse the fire.

When the last cinder glows weakly orange and dies she returns indoors and hears the faint sounds of her daughter's dreams.

Addy is awake. She lies in bed thinking of how Sister Christine had held up her handwriting book with the words, 'Sister Christine has grey-green eyes but she is not a cat,' inscribed in Addy's sensible, slanting hand, and in a shrill, icy tone had said:

'No one outside my family knows I have grey-green eyes... uhmmm. How did you know, my dear?'

'Adults, though they are adults,' Addy thinks, 'find it difficult to look us in the eye.'

Di turns in her troubled sleep and encounters a raven. He gazes at her intently and wags his head. He means the little girl well and asks where she is going all alone in the big wide world. How well she understands the word 'alone'. She tells the raven her whole story and asks if he has seen Kulay.

'Give the dress to Charity,' Ma hisses into her ear yet again, waking her out of her raggedy dreams.

When we were small we thought Charity was a girl. Addy and I. We thought Earthquake was a man rattling windows. We thought clothes grew small. We thought we could fly. Addy and I. We stood on the stone steps with our arms outstretched and prayed for the wind to blow us skywards. When we touched only ground we tried again. We carried bits of popcorn and five paisa sweets in little 'snack packets' and played all day long. When we went to shit it was like going to office. We said 'bye' to each other. The nine-to-five kind of bye.

We were kites. Clemmie, Addy and I. We were the pink, blue and red kites Kulay made every weekend until the day he disappeared. We stood next to him when he played kynteng with Martin, Terri and Revise from up the lane. We ran with him to grab an enemy kite captured at kynteng and we giggled and blushed about Martin, Terri and Revise from up the lane.

A HOME AND THE WORLD
(1984 - 1988)

12. DISSENT

Kulay is tired. He has been waiting for an hour now, listening to the banter around him at a rally organised by the Union in the football field opposite the mansion. He wipes the lime from a betel leaf with his forefinger and with it writes on the boundary wall the words: DON'T RUB LIME.

When he turns around, pin-drop silence has descended over the field. Lambert Narendra Don, the leader of the Union, has arrived. A huge applause assails him as he walks to the podium and turns to the crowd. But he is in no hurry. He looks at the sky. Kulay waits, not daring to breathe.

'This soil for its sons,' the leader declares suddenly. There is a clapping consensus.

'Get up and throw your weight around...,' shouts one of his aides. More clapping. More noise.

Snubbing him, Lambert Narendra Don now embarks upon his prepared speech.

'Our demands for equal employment opportunities have not been met by this government,' he says stressing his T's. 'There is gross discrimination against our people on every front. The border problem remains. The army continues to brutalise our brothers in neighbouring states. Does the central government think it can appease us by showing our songs and dances on national television?'

Kulay keeps his eyes glued on the man. A stone goes whizzing past his eyes. He blinks hard, but stones are flying in all directions. Lambert Narendra Don goes on speaking as the crowd breaks up in different directions searching for the *dkhars* who have attacked. Martin and Terri bash up four bystanders.

Kulay detaches himself from the crowd. For the first time since he left the mansion five years ago, for the first time since the resin fires burnt in celebration of his freedom, he is face-to-face with the house again.

He looks over his shoulder to see what has become of the mansion. It seems to him that the manor is beckoning him again, shedding tears of peeling paint for the boy it has lost. He peers hard at the portentous exterior of the house and wonders if that is May staring, according to her old hangover habit, out of the parlour window.

May is indeed gazing out of her parlour window, the greed and gumption on her face replaced now by a faraway look of neither love nor longing, but a split desire for everything and nothing.

When she comes to herself, she wonders if that was not Kulay disappearing beneath an Indian army truck. She gathers herself together and tries to rid herself of the illusion, for she often hallucinates that she is face-to-face with Kulay again as the stony lad demands to settle a score or two with her.

'Sexy tyres,' Kulay says to himself, raising the flap behind the truck. 'Sexy.'

He crawls under the truck as he spots a cop looking in his direction from across the road. He has been on the run ever since the day of the demonstration outside the St. James' gates, the school being in the forefront of the agitation. Lying under the truck, Kulay shivers with pleasure and dread at the memory of what had transpired on that day, exactly two years after he left the mansion.

The year was 1981. Father Gregarious had locked the school gates but some of the protestors had mounted them.

'Give us uniforms,' Kulay demanded with a tremor in his voice. He was feeling like a bundle of firewood, ready to set the streets on fire. After all, he was now a member of the Union.

The crowd boiled over. The men were armed with hockey sticks. But boys like Martin, Terri, Revise and Kulay were bolder. They carried iron chains and petrol bombs.

District Commissioner Manic Roy arrived in a white Ambassador car just in time to watch Kulay hit the air with clenched fists.

'Give us uniforms,' Kulay repeated.

Manic Roy narrowed his eyes and wondered what May's boy was doing in the midst of the mob.

'Go home, Kulay,' he tapped the agitator on the shoulder.

Kulay turned around and bit into his hand drawing blood. Manic Roy clamped down the teeth marks with his impeccably white handkerchief and ordered the armed police convoy to move in and arrest the boys —only the Khasi boys.

'Arrest me first,' said Father Gregarious, stepping in calmly between the boys and the convoy. Kulay squinted at the principal of St. James. He could not understand why this *dkhar* was inviting trouble.

Father Gregarious put his hand on Manic's shoulder. 'By arresting these boys you are encouraging them to rebel. Try and understand why they are angry.'

Father Gregarious, who counselled the local youth, was sympathetic to the demands of the Union. He tried to explain to Manic Roy that the boys had to be dealt with calmly. 'If you don't listen now, there will be no end to this violence. What we need is dialogue. The government has to stop being arrogant,' he said a little self-consciously but earnestly.

'This is a law-and-order issue,' Manic said coldly. He had been on the verge of ordering a lathi charge on the defiant boys for he believed himself to be an immutable object of power.

May had herself affirmed his power one languorous August afternoon, as she reclined on her sumptuous sofa, fragmented and supine. It had been raining non-stop for three days but the downpour had relented for a bit and the sun suggested itself in tiny glints that darted off Manic Roy's gold watch. He was watching May read *Macbeth* with only the silver tea service between them. May was reading disconsolately and aloud:

> Be lion-mettled, proud; and take no care
> Who chafes, who frets, or where conspirers are:
> Mac...Manic...

(She flattered charmingly.)

> Mac Manic shall never vanquish'd be until
> Great Birnam wood to high Dunsinane hill
> Shall come against him.

The absurd truth was that Manic believed her, which is why he couldn't quite believe his eyes when he now saw the woods begin to move.

The woods in this case were the cryptomarias and deodars that lined The Heart of Jesus Girls' High School that stood opposite St. James. Boys from the Union had already crossed the threshold and, beneath the statute of the Virgin Mary installed atop the convent chapel, intimated the school girls of a possible confrontation with the cops. The girls had broken off the leafy arms of the stately trees and were now advancing in visible defiance of Section 144.

They crossed the square in a blue-grey uniformed tide and swooped down between the lathis and the boys.

Kulay spied, amidst the uniformed sea, the face of a girl he had watched for sometime. He had often reached the square at 8 a.m. just to watch her pass the square and cross over to The Heart of Jesus. He hadn't, like the other boys, whistled or teased. He hadn't done anything. Just sat on the pavement and watched. She would keep her bag in class and reappear. She would buy *aloo moorri* and, while paying the hawker, glance at Kulay. Casually. Over her shoulder.

Kulay burnt fire-engine red. And burnt fire-engine red again when he spied her in the uniformed sea. He knew about the dkhar dog sniffing about her school skirt and knew that she consented to attention, irrespective of caste, community or colour.

This was dangerous. This was very, very dangerous.

He jumped over the locked school gates and raced towards the imposing concrete.

He ran up the staircase, spilling over with piss and sweet wrappers, up, up like a kite of his own invention and further up still ran the boy as the nostalgia of past glories rushed through his nose.

Finally, on the fifth floor, having thrown the graffitied desks and kicked the broken benches, having crossed himself before a marble Christus Rex and devoured the chalk, he stopped and gazed through the many-coloured window at the crowd below and a statue above.

Strong, athletic, heroic. Severe, resolute, romantic. The child of the sun, the kite-flier, mynja maker and resin burner looked out at a many-coloured world.

He looked past a simple iron grill enclosing the grey coloured statue of a man and two boys. The stone plaque was blurred from his vision but he knew it declared:

St. James—Educator and Benefactor of Youth

He looked past this man and past the moving wood to the winter-hazed sky. Its singular colour calmed him immensely. He could see Father Gregarious arguing vehemently with Manic Roy who wanted to break open the gates and have him arrested.

He stood there feeling a chill in his spine, until Father Gregarious had appeased Manic Roy and the crowd dispersed peacefully.

Lying under the army truck Kulay feels the same chill creeping up his spine. He has seen what becomes of the Union boys who are arrested. Despite the bravery he feels in his heart, he knows he must avoid an arrest. He slips out from under the truck and sees May at the parlour window.

May sees an apparition come towards her. She gathers herself together but the illusion persists. She sees it advancing slowly towards her.

'Ai Kulay...' she whispers, trying to grasp the boy in a childlike adult way.

Kulay's hands remain at his sides.

'I'm tired of running. Very, very tired,' he says.

It was 1984 '...and the clocks were striking thirteen...'.

13. INDEPENDENCE DAY

'Deeeee... Are you coming to my house?' Clemmie calls out.

A fourteen year old girl bolts through the forget-me-not hedge and runs towards the mansion as fast as her long legs can carry her. From the corner of her eye she sees the cagey smile spread across the face of the garage, but she runs past it swiftly. Time has flown since the day of the storm five years ago.

Phoebe is sitting at May's dressing table in her sports dress. Lovely Phoebe, all of twenty-two.

'Come and brush my hair.' She gives me her blue brush with the golden handle. Pretty, just like her.

'Your hair is silky, Phoebe.'

'No, it's like a broom. Brush it hard. Harder.'

I concentrate on Phoebe. What makes her so pretty? Is it her eyes, which twinkle when she laughs?

'I have to wash my clothes now,' Phoebe slips out her head from under the brush and smiles at me.

I put back the brush on the dressing table and go out even though I could have stayed there forever.

'Next year, I and Di will be in class nine,' Clemmie says.

'Di and I,' Addy corrects her. She is getting ready to go to class ten—the senior-most class of school.

Addy, Clemmie and I are waiting for Governor to come and pick us up from school.

'When will Governor stop fetching us?' I am craving to walk back home alone like Phoebe with her long hair dancing in a red-ribboned ponytail... walking and laughing in the sun.

'Perhaps next year Governor won't come to fetch us anymore,' Clemmie becomes pensive.

'We'll walk home like Phoebe with our friends and act big.'

'We won't act big,' Addy contradicts. 'We'll *be* big.'

Governor comes speeding up through the school gate honking at Clemmie. He does a roundabout turn in the driveway and halts right next to us. He leans back and opens the rear door.

Clemmie rushes in. Then Addy. Then... I.

'You have a holiday tomorrow,' Governor says.

'Why?' Addy asks

'Because it's Independence Day.'

'We'll go to the lake,' Clemmie whispers to me.

'No, we'll make flags,' Governor says overhearing her. He does not seem to understand that we have grown up. He narrows his eyes until they become little slits. The Ambassador smells of liquor.

Governor has been drinking inside the car all day. He started in the morning, the moment he spied May leaving the mansion. Unlike the earlier days, he did not ask her where she was going. He already knew. He had known it five years ago and found himself smouldering in the flame that had flickered steadily in her heart all these years. This was the longest she had been enamoured of any man.

May is surprised at herself. Perhaps she is growing old. But Benji (for Benjamin is Benji to her now) has taken long to relent. And she is still not sure he is entirely hers.

She traces her finger over his broad chest. It is a broad chest after all. Broader than she had thought. Quite hairless for a *dkhar*.

'They say you were a priest, Benji.'

'They say you are a princess.'

Always elusive. A slightly nasal voice. Courteous even when intimate.

'I know Shillong backwards, Ma'am.' He is eager to impress upon her his oneness with the land.

'Doesn't impress me,' she shoots back stylishly. 'I have never felt... y'know... a part of the tribe.'

He strikes a match. The smoke tickles her throat.

'Huh.'

'I've been mistreated. I tried to rebel. That's it. It's my way of rebelling.'

He is secretly happy she has said that. Perhaps he is relieved.

'I want to leave the mansion.'

'Why?'

'I'm scared of... the boy... of... everything.' She tries to look at him winsomely.

'...and I really want to be closer to you.'

'What about Clemmie?' he asks, startled at his own concern for May's exquisite daughter.

'What about Clemmie?' she echoes.

Once May goes home firmer in her resolve to leave the mansion, Benji's thoughts return to the previous Sunday when he had visited the mansion.

Clemmie's eyes had stared straight into his as he stood embracing May that spineless Sunday morning.

They were meant to be in Church, but Governor being away in the village and it being a sinful-smelling Sunday, they had decided to stay indoors but had forgotten to lock the door.

Clemmie, good old, religious Clemmie, had washed her hair with three buckets of water, put on her white smocked dress and was searching for her Bible. The singing had begun and the bells tolled blatantly from the nearby church tower.

'Knock, and I shall open each door,' Clemmie sang in a high falsetto as she walked into May's sitting room without knocking.

Two pairs of eyes collided. One pair was sinking into the coral pink arms of silk that were opening up to them. But they shot out of the mesmerising pink at the sound of the door, like two startled children, and crashed into a pair of eyes that was worried, wise and very, very old.

'Clemmie-Clemmie, we're coming to your house.'

After the announcement, Addy and I proceed through the hedge on the morning of Independence Day.

I hold Addy's hand but she pushes it away.

Governor is standing outside the garage sawing a bamboo pole. 'Make a flag,' Governor says, shaving the pole. 'Make a flag and raise it from the roof.'

Clemmie refuses to make one but Addy and I feel obliged to get busy.

'Get the sticky rice from May's pot,' Governor commands, raising the bamboo pole. 'Get the sticky rice to stick the flag.'

May sits presiding over the pots in the dark kitchen where the sun never goes.

'There's going to be a fight,' May says, chewing her *kwai* viciously. She is cutting carrots that are immersed in a bowl of water. 'There's going to be a fight between the *dkhars* and the Khasis, so you better watch out.'

Energised by the flag-hoisting ceremony, Governor storms indoors. The kitchen appears to shrink under the sound of his foreboding footsteps. A tin saucepan clatters to the floor. May looks up from the carrots, startled.

'A glass of wine, May? A glass of wine to celebrate our independence?' He grins, upturning the bowl full of carrots and water onto May's lap.

Curiosity-the-cat leaps off the kitchen table in fright.

May eyes him doubtfully. Has stupid Clemmie said something she shouldn't have?

'Not that I care,' she says aloud, trying to gather herself together.

'I happen to be allergic to Sabbath...' Governor begins, drawing a wooden stool forward. He trails off seeing Kulay enter, shouldering an axe.

Kulay thrusts a handful of splintered wood into the fire. It blazes up radiantly.

'More.'

May notices Kulay picking up the dark green bottle of local liquor from under the kitchen sink.

'More wood.'

Kulay walks out without a word.

'And I didn't interfere with your plans when you decided to take him back.' Governor nods in the direction of Kulay's receding back.

'I?!'

That shuts him up. He scrapes the stool noisily and storms out, shivering in anger.

An uneasy air of compromise descends over the household restoring its frangible harmony.

On the afternoon of Independence Day, I sneak through the hedge to see the flag flying crookedly over May's red roof.

Kulay is sitting on the lawn with his grim back towards me.

'Hi,' Kulay almost smiles. He hands me an empty bottle. 'Can you put this in the garage... please?' He does not bully.

I run the errand for his sake.

It is quiet inside the garage.

Hopefully, Governor is out.

But when I turn around, he is standing behind me. He is wearing his broad-brimmed cowboy hat. When he shuts the garage door behind me, I see Kulay like a faraway speck in the sky.

Then everything turns dark and throbs.

'Governor...' May tears open the garage door.

I stop kicking and fighting. Governor lets go of my dress. He strolls past

May casually as she stares at him in shock. He walks nonchalantly into the distance and after a while looks over his shoulder to see if she has gone. May is rooted to the spot unable to move or speak.

I slither out of the garage not knowing where I am going.

Benji recalls the particular circumstances leading up to the eye crash again and again. He feels her eyes floating up to his and then unwittingly interlocked in utter shock. How can she make him feel the guilt he has always evaded, he wonders.

He sits up all night on the broken stone wall around his villa at the rear of Bernard's. The smell of pumpkin pie crumbs, which Clemmie occasionally drapes around herself, lingers tremulously in the air.

He sits watching the luminous crescent of the moon. Who am I, he wonders. And what, precisely, do I want?

On Independence Day, many things decide to become independent of each other and declare their autonomy.

'By prying into my life, you cannot make me love you anymore. But let us be civil strangers,' concludes an unexpected note to Ma.

For a moment she cannot understand why it is addressed to her but she remembers all too soon. This is a sign, she fears. It is a sign of worse news to come. She wishes she could share her fears with May but her landlady seems lost in her own thoughts.

Ma does not know that May has finally decided to leave the mansion.

'I am leaving because I want you gone from my life,' May tells Governor, oblivious of the fact that the object of her desires is contemplating a retreat.

'I won't be... coming... anymore. But... send Clemmie to me... sometimes... I'll... help her get along... Ma'am.' Benji puts down his thoughts on paper but folds the letter to May and for the time being puts it away.

14. THE RIOT

Kulay watches her dusty feet advance towards him in the kind of rubber sandals May would never wear. Redcoat wears a maroon pout and seems to have bangles instead of forearms, fourteen clinking silver bangles.

> Rings on her fingers
> And bells on her toes
> We shall have music wherever she goes.

She appears to be coming towards him but changes her mind and walks out of the mansion gate. He follows her but does not go into Solomon's Mines.

May watches a stooping seventeen year old Kulay disappear into the distance from her parlour window. Her heart misses a beat. She has often tried to meet his restless grey eyes. She thinks of the golden stubble trembling on his chin.

Unlike the earlier days when he resented doing the chores she assigned him but did them anyway, he has refused to do any work since he returned. May feels frustrated at the thought that she hasn't been able to coerce him as she could once do.

She contemplates taking him to her new house. 'Take him there and tell him. But then... where can I begin?' She sits motionless, shrunken.

Often she would mistake a boy on the street for Kulay and begin to say something.

'I must leave,' she thinks, fearing for her sanity.

Kulay keeps walking until something arrests his attention.

In a street corner of the town, inconspicuous by itself, but made remarkable now by the presence of a very gaudy Goddess, a group of young men have gathered to complete their cycle of worship by immersing an idol of the

Goddess Kali in the river. Joss sticks have burnt into her body. She wears wilted flowers around her neck.

Kulay stares at her long and hard, simultaneously keeping an eye on the Police Beat House for he suspects Manic Roy has issued a warrant for his arrest and they can come for him any time.

The last time they came for him he had been drinking tea at Solomon's Mines with Martin and Terri. It was Redcoat who had given the eye to the Central Reserve Police Force duo lingering outside the shop.

They entered casually, and casually, Martin and Terri slipped away. Kulay inched towards the door. He broke into an unhurried run, ducking behind the Mohammedans who were making their way to the mosque where the Friday prayers would soon begin.

As he ran, he feared the famed Central Reserve Police Force *lathi* might catch him between his legs. They had a special skill of obstructing a runner with a strategically angled *lathi*. Kulay almost tripped at the thought. He decided he must give up smoking, for his lungs hurt a great deal.

'There is no such thing as a soft arrest,' Lambert Narendra Don had once told the Union on his release from jail. Lambert Narendra Don had been beaten up so badly he was soft in the head. He had kept repeating that there was no such thing as a soft arrest.

Kulay crawled between the worshippers heading towards the mosque. They smelt strange, he thought, but felt safe within their faithful legs. When they reached the gates of the mosque, he got back on his feet and walked into the grassy lawns where hundreds of knees were bending and hundreds of heads turned in prayerful unison. As Kulay joined them he realised that his heart was fluttering in its cage.

'There is really no such thing as a soft arrest,' he thought.

Kulay is watching Ma Kali intently now. Perhaps the serpent coiled at her feet has turned her blue in the face. His eyes travel over her braids. A garland of severed heads adorns her bold neck. He stands there transfixed. Then slowly he moves towards the primeval Goddess and nudges her gently to see if she will speak.

'...*When the idols of Ma Kali were being lifted for immersion within yards of the Police Beat House, a young man, belonging to another community, trying to make a short cut, contemptuously crossed over the idol and the idol was broken...*'

'Look at that crowd,' says Governor, peering over *The Shillong Weekly*, across the stone wall that runs along the mansion. A huge crowd has gathered in the football field to protest against the false accusations levied by the *dkhars* against a Union boy. 'A fly can't fart in that damn crowd.'

'Aiee Governaar!' EverComfort Son, who is standing among the villagers recruited for the occasion, calls out to Governor asking him to join them.

Governor pretends not to have heard him. The butcher-brother congratulates him loudly for joining hands with the oppressors.

He has arrived from his village in an overcrowded bus, soaked in rice beer and passion. Lambert Narendra Don, who has now begun to slur, thanks to the police beatings, will soon address the swelling rally.

Lambert Narendra Don clears his husky throat and congratulates the people for 'being prepared to shed blood for their motherland.'

He explains why the Union has unleashed its violence on the town.

When May, leaving Clemmie to fret over Kulay, joins Governor at the wall, Lambert Narendra Don is opposing the extension of railway lines into the town, which, if allowed, will encourage people from outside to engulf Shillong.

Then, turning in the direction of the mansion and booming into the loudspeaker, Lambert Narendra Don asserts that some non-tribals are purchasing land in the name of their tribal friends in Shillong.

'The tribals,' he says, staring threateningly at May and Governor, who are watching him from their boundary wall, 'are conniving with these non-tribals.'

There is a ringing silence during which a pall of gloom descends over the mansion and entangles itself in the smoke from the chimney of that unhappy home.

'The existence of our people is at stake,' says the leader, 'fight now or be wiped out.' And with those words, he steps down from his perch and lets loose the eager crowd.

It is Addy who first spies the smoke coming out of the Bihari Brothers' shop. She fears the worst as she watches vast columns of smoke gushing through the chimney. Perhaps the Brothers Grimm are cooking up something in those big black pots.

'I wish. I wish,' she thinks and her thighs begin to ache with wishing, for nothing exciting ever happens except in books.

Curiosity-the-cat appears on the windowsill and begins to lick her paws. She leaps down from the windowsill on to Addy's aching thighs and from there on to the satin cushions where she curls up herself and goes to sleep.

And still the smoke is rising and again Addy fears the worst is going to happen as she now spies a mob of angry men coming towards the mansion.

'You have no spirit, May,' cries the mob in one voice when they reach the mansion's gate after setting the Bihari Brothers' shop alight. They demand that the dkhar family May is hiding be produced before them.

'She has cent percent spirit,' replies Governor, as he puts a heavy drunken arm on May's rapidly shrinking shoulders for she has grown very frightened and very brave indeed. 'What is your percentage?' Governor himself has turned into Tiny Tim and his face is brown and wrinkled.

'We want the family you are hiding,' cry the mob in unison. Governor draws May closer than he ever has and ever will and whispers something into her ear.

'I will send them to you but not one toe shall touch my Hilarious property,' May mumbles and hurries away, leaving Governor to mute the united voice.

'Your leader is half *dkhar*, born in a foreign country,' says Governor, adding fuel to fire and laughing in fright.

'You are a traitor,' retorts the voice, growing sharp with impatience.

'At least I was born on the soil of Shillong,' quips the sentry of the mansion, hoping that the To-Lets have been evacuated by this time.

'The Punjabis have Punjab, the Bengalis have Bengal but we only have this little land,' shouts the voice, unwilling to tolerate the traitor any longer.

When Di joins Addy at the window of their little house it is evident to them that the blaze below has been started by very angry people indeed.

Agitated voices drift across May's well-tended lawns and over her red bougainvillea camber into their trembling ears.

'Let there be blood and death,' cry the women of the mob.

The church tower bells that chime to tell the people in town of every service are now silent and wistful.

May hurries towards the forget-me-not hedge. She charges through the hedge with an iron will despite the growing clamour.

The To-Lets are at the window in full strength by this time. The blaze rising from May's rented row of shops below illuminates the translucent orange trees so that the fruit appears even more thin-skinned than it is, and threatens to smite the onlookers with its succulence.

Ma joins the girls at the window. Is that him in the crowd?

She looks again at the street though her daughters beg her not to do so lest they draw the attention of the irate mob, which does not seem to be in a particularly merciful mood.

Ignoring them, Ma inches closer to the window to get a better view.

There he is, she thinks, studiously avoiding the To-Let House for he must know that I live here. Perhaps he has expected her to move on. Instead she has chosen to stay right where he left her. He must feel compromised, thinks Ma. He must hope that she will not call his bluff, that if they become civil strangers, she will hesitate to speak out. He has no idea that I have been hurt into silence, she thinks, he does not wish to have much of an idea anyway.

Ma wants to know whose side he is on. Perhaps he has fooled the Union members too. Perhaps the Union members, not foot soldiers, but more middle-aged men who have seen it all, have nodded circumspectly chewing ferociously on their *kwai*, as he tried to talk to them about good and bad protest. Perhaps they've even asked him to help them write their manifesto. Perhaps the doors of the elite have finally begun to open for him.

'Anyway.' He must surely have snapped his fingers and dismissed her from his mind. Forgetting her must have been as easy as snapping his fingers, she thinks bitterly.

They have surely invited him for the demonstration. A smile, not inaccurately oleaginous, must have spread across his face, she thinks. Then they must have described to him the political contours of the demonstration and he must have relished the carnival-like details. As the men put their heads together, a heady smell of chewed *kwai* and tobacco must have crept out of their mouths, pleasurably tickling his senses.

Perhaps there are happy domestic sounds coming from his kitchen. Perhaps a woman in an apron is singing as she cooks. Perhaps she has told him that very morning that he makes a splendid husband. Emerging from the kitchen, she, maybe, puts her arm around him and bends her head to look at the demonstration plans. And perhaps then, the *dkhar* in him is temporarily quelled.

Ma tries to open the window and shout out a curse at the man whom she suspects is him. She cannot believe he has gone so native that he has donned a full indigenous dress. She thinks she sees him swaying a little self-consciously to the beating of the drums that accompany the angry mass.

As Ma struggles to open the window, her crying daughters pull her back, imploring her to think about their safety. So strong is the force of this tug-of-war, that the To-Lets collapse in a little heap on the floor as the battle rages on outside their endangered home.

May enters in her horribly high heels. The To-Lets disentangle themselves and rise from the floor.

'Hide!' she cries frantically.

The voice of the protestors bursts through the walls of the mansion.

Ma protests as May brings down a big black cloth upon her head. 'They'll ransack the house and burn you alive,' May says, urging a curious-shaped black cloth with three pairs of legs to proceed towards the coal store in the backwaters of the mansion. Midway, however, Ma furtively lifts the cloth and slips out from under it.

The smoke from the blaze in the Bihari Brothers shop has begun to merge with the smoking effigy of the Chief Minister, which Kulay recklessly helps burn at the St. James Square.

Dr J J Sintar, the Chief Minister, has requested the Union not to give the *dkhars* a raw deal.

'This man must go,' say the leaders of the Union and they thrust his effigy into the blaze that is licking the iron grill enclosing the grey coloured statue of a man and two boys.

The sound of the somniferous drums reaches Kulay from the depths of the blue hill ranges. The agitators on the other side have begun to beat them ominously.

'Lambert Narendra Don,' Terri tells Kulay in the midst of the chaos, 'owns a fleet of vehicles and is a moron.'

'He walks crookedly,' jeers Kulay as he mimes the Big Boss' police-stricken walk.

They are walking away from the square now like Soldiers of the Cross, dividing the burden of their rice beer between them. They talk excitedly as they move towards the church behind the square where more dissenters are beating the ancient drums.

But Kulay isn't listening anymore for he is dreaming that he has replaced Lambert Narendra Don and is standing at the people's pulpit doing his utmost for the hallowed tribe. They applaud him enthusiastically as he towers above them. On and on he speaks, until his speech wafts above his head surpassing the thin frame of the passionate boy.

He feels a great tragic sense of the land for which he is fighting.

For the last five years Kulay had been learning things from the chaos he had embraced. He had done time in the poorest villages, among the men who gathered in the evenings at the common drinking stalls.

'What kind of wind blows you here, young man?'

But they were not hostile. He had never spoken, only listened to the many conversations.

'Come and meet my family,' a man had laid his toiling hand upon Kulay's shoulder.

He had slept in fields and in moving trucks. The muted wails of village children brought a great sense of responsibility into his heart.

After all, he would be the only one to venture back into that world where destinies were presided over. And though he knew that their lives, in the final sense, were woven out of their own will, and that they were inviolable by him or the Union, an almost paternal anxiety overwhelmed him when he re-entered the town and returned to the mansion.

Would he be able to carry out the promises he had silently made to them? Would he be able to lead them from the dark villages, where electricity had not yet reached, into the blazingly lit world of plenty? Would they take him seriously? How would he take from the rich and give to the poor when his brothers were so abysmally divided among themselves?

Kulay now sees it clearly in his reverie. The land – his land – lies blistered by cracks and deluges and imaginary red and blue lines that divide it into several desiccated pieces. His vision is of the sixteen huts from which his people are believed to have come. He hopes they can be raised to heaven on the branches of the golden oak vine again.

He does not hear the people cry that the golden bridge between heaven and earth is broken, for sin has covered the world and all they can be sure of is that this golden boy will, as other golden boys must, 'like chimney sweepers come to dust'.

Her clothes flapping wildly behind her, Ma bursts through the crowd that has gathered at the mansion. She makes straight for his face with a knife that she has so far concealed in her fist. Before he can speak a steady trickle of blood bursts out from the two crosses she has cut across his face. A loud cry of agony emanates from the depths of his being.

But this is not the man she thought he was. This is absolutely not her man.

She feels sorry now that she has accomplished her minor revenge. She feels so unspeakably grieved. She has no thought of the danger she is in.

The agitators have been taken by surprise and for a moment freeze in disbelief at the violence of the act that the silent woman has committed.

Addy and Di continue towards May's coal stores under the big black cloth. For a little while they are unaware of Ma's escape but when they realise she has disappeared, they are paralysed with fear.

Their life in the town has turned precarious.

Di is thinking of the lake. Even if there is no place in the world left to go to, Di believes the lake will have her. She knows people go there when they have nowhere left to go. The lake opens out its arms and swallows them. She knows it will blissfully swallow her if she asks it to.

Ma's innocent victim sinks to the ground a little comically. His stomach sags limply above the colourful loincloth. His legs melt beneath him and lie askew on the ground. The feathers from his fantastic headgear are crushed under the weight of his unconscious head. His arms stretch out above his head in the pose of a surrendered soothsayer.

As a few women from the mob break off to tend to him, the rest of the people pull themselves together and begin to chase Ma, who, having also come to herself, has broken into a run suddenly cognisant of the danger she has invited.

Knowing the ins and outs of the mansion, her two feet transport her in a flash to the coal store even as the multitude scatter themselves here and there over May's property, looking high and low for the bizarre *dkhar* woman so that they might punish her for the uncalled-for crime.

Ma bursts into the coal store and fiercely locking the door behind her, peers at her whimpering daughters. They are frightened to their fingers and are holding each other in a great greasy hug.

Ma stares hard at the coal, as another frenzied horde detonates through the gates and enters the mansion in search of the *dkhars* who have been hidden by the most hated woman in Shillong.

May has produced a Bible and is swearing by it now.

'The *dkhar* children are busy studying,' she scolds, 'while you make trouble with the tribal kids.'

As Addy overhears this, she realises with horror that her career stands imperilled by the recent event.

'What will happen to my future?' she asks tugging at Ma's sari. She is sure that the future has turned into the first page of her *Story of Creation* book.

It is very, very dark.

As Ma stares at the heaps of coal, May is placing an unringed finger on the velvet coverlet of her Bible.

Ma crawls towards a heap and worms her way beneath it. She pushes with such energy that the whimpering girls fear she might sink into the adamantine earth. Pieces of coal tumble over her head. An ember dust enters her mouth.

'No more exploitation and oppression of our people,' shouts the mob.

Governor is trying to hold up a section of the crowd by a bombastic speech on the Indian flag, which they spy flying crookedly from the roof of the mansion and demand to denigrate.

'Three decades since Independence but we Indians have got a lot to learn about how to display a national flag on a national day,' says Governor, as he stands between the crowd and the flag.

'We will fly the flag in sewage trucks and on roof tops of latrines,' says the voice of the mob, which is now reaching Ma's ears as she makes a desperate attempt to wriggle beneath the obscuring mineral.

'This is against the provisions of the flag code,' says the man whose own flag is flying wrong side up and has turned from tri-colour to multi-colour in the rain.

Addy is crying in earnest.

Ma is crying on the floor.

Di is crying.

Governor who has learnt that you cannot start a sentence with 'because' rather late in life, has now run out of reasons to keep the mob at bay and is overpowered by the hundreds who say they are 'avengers' and have come to make amends.

They run to and fro over the mansion grounds with joyous shouts but cannot locate the family of three who have crawled inside the coal coloured earth and are now trembling with the celerity of an earthquake.

Clemmie opens the brass-knobbed door of the mansion and peers through it with one eye closed. She is worried sick about Kulay.

The golden lad is at this point squinting in the light from the Church's stained glass windows. He knows he, and only he, can replace Lambert Narendra Don and make the supreme sacrifice. Perhaps this will entitle him to live in a palace where the floors are made of crystal, the doors of solid gold.

An appalling love for the land and its people balloons in his ears. Ignoring a skinny clerk, who is making a speech with the full force of his wiry frame, Kulay enters the church and stands looking at its marble tablets and brass plates for a long while.

His blood, however, begins to sour as he spots armoured vehicles, with men masked in black, beginning to rove the inner arena.

The mob wanes as quickly as it has waxed and the mansion falls silent.

May thrusts her unringed fingers through the window of the coal store and hands the trembling trio three half cups of tea. As Addy sips the reviving brew she realises that, like the quality of mercy, it is not strained. The tea leaves irritate her tongue. She feels a shiver run down her spine. She wonders if her father has died in the riot.

The world changes colour, texture, interest and meaning according to the book she is reading.

15. BORDERLINE

A cold war crops up between May and Clemmie for the latter does not want to leave the mansion while the mother insists she must.

The shift also means a shift in schools.

'I'll have to go with her,' Clemmie whispers to me. 'She'll make me go with her and she'll make me change schools.'

'Why change schools?'

'Because Bernard's is nearer to the damn new house. Why don't you change too? Ask your mother.'

A shiver runs down Clemmie's spine. She shuts her eyes and awaits her removal from the familiar environs of Little Rose Convent.

May summons a horse-drawn cart to carry her belongings to her new home.

I stand at the stone wall and watch a small sooty boy in a man's coat guide the horse through the cars and go past the mansion gate. Then, hitting himself on the head, he retraces his steps and enters the driveway leading up to the mansion.

May stands watching him at the door. Phoebe exclaims at the cart, sweetly startled. She is preparing to leave soon too. She shall move to a bigger city and Sissy Kay will be shifted to a hostel.

The boy steps on May's crimson carpet. She screams at him and he slips off his broken shoes tiptoeing under the weight of his burden.

We help May pack her belongings.

I pause to peer at myself in the mirror in front of May's four-poster bed. I can see Phoebe flipping through a book. I watch closely for a resemblance between her and me but there is none.

'It's all for the new house,' May says. 'I never thought these curtains would ever come down... Phoebe.'

May arranges her unruly hair in the mirror and addresses Phoebe who is still reading.

In the bare room, May remembers scenes from her past. Conversations return like familiar music pieces. And in the midst of remembrance and regret, she thinks of Benji.

Benji stares again at the letter he has written to May. Then he retreats into a corner of his mind where he has hidden Clemmie and winks at her.

It is a magnificent hiding place.

As for his other secrets, they are mostly out in the open and some are in the cases under his bed where they make strange bedfellows with his school papers. He has led most people to believe that he had been a priest but left the fraternity before he arrived in Bernard's. He thinks it makes him enigmatic and fashionable.

His fingers gnaw at the undelivered letter. He wonders if there can be a safer place to hide Clemmie.

May prepares to leave the mansion one morning in autumnal September as the ten o'clock siren goes off in the air, much to the consternation of Shillong's office goers.

May leaves behind a boozy Governor and a white trembling son. Kulay approaches her as if to say goodbye but she shoves him away. She fears she is losing control of her mind for she no longer feels any hatred towards him. Only a slight pang where her hate once consumed her.

Ma is late for office but she stands weeping at the gate for her benefactress.

May sticks out her surprisingly slender hand and offers it to each of the To-Let trio. Then she is gone like a witch disappearing on her broom in a flurry of smoke. As the tail of May's vehicle disappears around the mansion's gate, Di finds her eyes turning to water even though Clemmie has promised a letter everyday.

In the new house, Clemmie passes her study table with her eyes tightly shut trying to block out from her vision the huge pile of books that has grown so lofty it is sure to fall.

She is busy cutting up pictures and making Christmas cards. But she is not looking forward to the New Year.

Benji fiddles with the letter in his pocket as he sits facing May, who has returned to his villa eager to tell him that she has settled into her new home and he is welcome to visit her.

Still something stops him from giving the letter to her just then.

'Alright,' he says, not unkindly, even though he has not quite heard what she has been saying.

He shifts the conversation as subtly as he can to Clemmie. Would she want some help in addition to her regular classes at Bernard's?

May goes to great lengths to explain to him how supremely unworthy of almost anything her daughter is.

He wonders if she resents Clemmie's astonishing beauty.

'I'll send her to you for help,' May opens her enchanting burgundy leather clutch to check if she has eaten her lipstick. 'Her future is in your hands,' she adds ominously as she clicks her purse shut.

Clutching her books Clemmie, who has been admitted into Bernard's, proceeds to Benji's villa at the rear of the school.

He spies her blurred face peeping through his window and his heart leaps up in its cage.

Clemmie stands reluctantly at the threshold and cannot remember where she has seen that look in his eyes before.

Of course she has seen him several times but there is one particular moment when she has seen that look in his eyes. She cannot remember where.

He offers her a chair. A clement smell of foreign tobacco enters through the window.

'Did May come and blah, blah, blah, again?' Clemmie asks, surprising herself at the easy manner in which she is able to strike up a conversation.

'Can... I can help you out?' says Benji, who is still awkward at forty and is grappling with a grand imprecise feeling that his life has not as yet begun.

He watches the poor little rich kid who has stumbled her way into his sylvan settings.

'Baby, I'll crack you the nut of exams,' he says. 'And then every time you'll be right no matter what.'

The girl in the dark green jeans is intrigued.

How mercilessly her fragrance tickles him.

'I'm borderline,' continues little Miss Innocently Insolent, gifting him up her troubled eyes.

Clemmie joins more who's-who daughters on her little scholarly missions. But Benji is ambiguous about these frequent visits to the villa. He is tormented by many doubts and fears.

The elms around the villa admit many young misguided heads and leading the pack is Little Miss Clemmie herself, thinner and taller now, her face hollowed out by harrowing encounters far beyond the capacity of her fifteen years.

Clemmie's wan cheeks redden a little when Benji's hand rests fondly on the bright black head that is working violently on a piece of unending algebra.

'What do people say about me, Clemmie, out there in the gay town beyond Benji-villa?'

'They ask why so many women in your house, Benji.'

'Ok. So what do you think I should do?'

'Why do you ask me? How should I know?'

He smarts a little at her cold retort. But this is not what he wants. There is more to this Clemmie, his Clemmie, he convinces himself.

For the moment, however, he gives her fifty equations and says: 'You better do them because they'll come in the exams no matter what.'

A few weeks later Benji starts persuading Clemmie to stay behind after her lessons in order to talk to her. Clemmie can listen for hours without once moving her tremulous eyelashes and then come up with the most incredible solutions. At least that is how he chooses to see them. He even implements some of what she suggests.

That isn't the point. The point is to enter her mind and make himself felt. Then he can become aware of the world as if, through Clemmie, he has been born into it again.

Her mathematical incompetence is endearing.

She has no idea what she is doing with maths anyway. She isn't cut out for maths. She cannot understand calculus. She just cannot. She grows hot and red at these moments and flutters her troubled eyelashes.

He is amazed at how different she is from May.

She is amazed at how different he is from anyone she has ever known.

For the first time in her life she has met someone, who will talk to her like a normal person. How unlike May who is either pampering or paranoid; how unlike Governor who is boisterous or drunk; how unlike Kulay who is distant and cold. How unlike anyone she has ever known. Talking to her. And not just talking but asking her opinions.

Ignoring the pounding in her head, Clemmie races down Jacob's ladder, the steps that offer a short cut home. She has had an exceptionally intense session at the villa and it is pitch dark by the time she leaves. She lunges forward into the stinking darkness and hears laughter and the sound of shattering glass.

A gang of boys is approaching her. She stands without breathing in the drain that runs along the side of the steps, waiting for the crowd to pass and recognises Kulay's voice thrown recklessly into the emptiness.

'Lambert Narendra Don—bastard number one.

Bob Marley—bastard number two.

Terri Turncoat—bastard number three. No more worthy bastards. Not even Kulay—the real bastard.'

And with each sentence Kulay smashes an empty bottle on the road and laughs like the devil he has outgrown.

At Benji's villa, varied flowers, born in the seasons of love and longing when May's love for him had been in its prime, are sunning themselves and dreaming their own dreams.

Several young boys and girls, with the fear of exams in their toes, have now begun to converge on Benji's little-visited villa. Among them is Revise, who has forsaken the Union and returned to his books.

Clemmie, Benji decides, is so utterly different from anyone that she has to be kept away, in a glass case, if need be.

'Don't do class with the other girls,' he suggests jealously. Clemmie is glad she doesn't have to. She does not know why he has decided that. But she is glad she has to do something entirely different alone.

She sits at the oblong cinnamon coloured desk that has many drawers.

Occasionally Revise enters the room and asks, 'Do you know how to solve this problem?'

And she replies, 'No.'

Meanwhile, the rest of the students sit in the adjoining room that has some worn-out kitchen tables, a blackboard, and a large mahogany armchair, all of which have been donated by May who is anxious to please the newly appointed tutor.

'Who's Di?' Benji asks, surprising Clemmie one day as she sits composing a letter to her friend instead of doing her sums. She leans ardently towards him trying to snatch back the letter. He sickens with absurd longings and gives her a sound spank.

'Who's Di?'

'Friend.'

'I didn't know you had friends.'

But there are far too many youngsters in the villa now. There is Helen the tart and other general act-smarts, and they snigger and whisper about Benji's crush on Clemmie.

'So what should I do about Helen?'

'Maybe you should do this, this, this,' says Clemmie, feeling intensely proud that he has consulted her, yet trying to be indifferent.

'But if I do this, then this will happen.'

They are in his room.

'Can we go out please?'

Despite his overt fondness for Clemmie, Benji is scared he will turn into the laughing stock of the town if he continues to seek her out publicly. He has never been able to shrug off the sniggers he imagines the town folk indulge in behind his back.

He had lived with this sense of being ridiculed even during his early days as a Bernardian teacher, when sickened of the contradictions within the institution, he had been on the verge of leaving. But he was grounded. Unable to gather enough momentum to take flight, unable to soar.

He had almost left once. He had stood inside his room with his bags packed, staring out onto the desolate field where the boys gathered to play cricket in the evenings.

He had noticed the Rector leave his office and walk towards a woman and her child. The child looked up eagerly at the Rector and he bent down to touch her cheek. Then, foolishly, he raced with the child, throwing out a ball and crying, 'catch... catch.'

The Rector having distracted the child with the ball was edging away from her. Away from her and towards the woman and slowly they were moving away—strolling casually at first, then disappearing into the shadows of the building cast by the setting sun.

He stared long and hard at the buildings.

In one of those rooms... he thought, in one of those rooms... known to me but unknown to the child who is still trying to throw the ball into the net while the setting sun blinds her eyes.

Benji had watched unmoving, stunned by the lust that was seeking cover. He had almost left then.

Then slowly, his mouth had spread into a wide, wicked smile.

That night, he had surreptitiously visited the Principal's office.

The Rector had not been seen after that day.

A similar smile forms on his lips as he recalls this incident. His fears about Clemmie seem to snuggle into his smile. His desire to leave abates. He can stay on, he tells himself. He can stay right here as long as he, unlike the Rector he once knew, can keep his little secret.

16. ARRESTED

The mansion wears a hungry look after May's departure.

Ma, who wakes up with the first streaks of light, often notices Redcoat walking across the lawns of the house. She has assumed an air befitting the first lady of the mansion, as she washes and wrings dry Kulay's clothes, propping up the clothesline with a bamboo pole until it almost measures up to the red roof of the mansion.

One day Ma notices Redcoat thrashing wildly at the forget-me-not hedge. She has managed to persuade Governor to build a boundary wall dividing the respectable front part of the house from its shabby backyard.

When a wall looms up between the mansion and the To-Let House only the tree of May's prophecy is visible.

Looking at this tree, May would often say, 'If the branches bend east the Chinese Army will invade us. That's what Clemmie's Granny told me when I was little.'

'If it sprouts new leaves, that'll be a good sign,' Phoebe had continued laughing up at the tree gaily.

'But if its branches dry up...?' Kulay questioned. 'Ruin-Ruin,' Sissy Kay had shrieked, running helter-skelter in that innocent summer a very long time ago.

The year that saw Kulay return to the mansion is almost coming to an end. In the winter of 1984, a month after May has left the mansion, Kulay strolls towards a bus requisitioned to drive around town with slogan-shouting supporters of the Union. He has been going hungry for the second day now but he does not care.

He drifts along listlessly with Martin and Terri.

He is thinking of his crystal palace. He pines for it, for he believes it is his true home. The lights are too dim for him here and the sun sets below the horizon.

In the palace, it is possible to hear the most beautiful sounds, like the sound of a nightingale in the witching hour of night. Perhaps, Kulay thinks languidly, Terri, his page boy, might bow to him and say, 'Lord of the Sun, Master of the Moon and Stars, the brown bird of the forest has come to sing to you.'

Ma hears the droning of Redcoat's lawnmower on the other side of the wall. She feels sounds entering her ears anew. The colour of the orange trees blisters her eyes. Brand new smells enter her nose suddenly intoxicating her.

There is a spring in her step as she prepares for office that morning.

After her miraculous escape from the wrath of the mob, Ma has returned to the To-Let House feeling giddily on the edge of life. Nothing lasts, she declares to herself, not unhappily that morning. For once she has not been woken by the aching alarm that is embedded inside her. For once she has not dreamt of him.

Something has been lifted from her heart. A feeling of impermanence has replaced the millstone of grief. Everything now appears to her to be constituted of very evanescent things indeed.

When Ma reaches her office, Moishree Ditto's father, the chief accountant at the Conservation Centre, is poking his fingers into the fallen stitches of his sweater and speculating in a safe and general way about the atrocities that each community committed during the riots.

'She was my wife's friend,' he says, heaving a sigh.

He is talking about a woman who was murdered during the riots. She was heavily pregnant when they led her out of her house on the hills and shoved a bamboo pole up her thighs. The only resistance they encountered was from her husband who could not keep his eyes open.

A stony, seventeen year old boy wrenched open the man's eyelids. Just in time for him to see her being heaved onto a tree and look enormously ridiculous as she fluttered her naked arms like a diminished angel and died.

'This is what I escaped,' quivers Ma for incidents like these had occurred in the light of day and in full public view on that fateful day of the riot.

Kulay relives the scene again.

He had never set his eyes on a thing like this before. He hung on to it as if it was his life blood. He had forced himself to participate in the public torture of the unfortunate woman, even though his abdomen churned at the spectacle. He kept his eyes wide open and when he returned to the mansion threw up a good amount of guilt in May's washbasin.

The riot and its fallout have revived his interest in the Union now.

He decides to attend every public meting out of justice taking place in town. His head is full of fine and foolish ideas when he faces the semi-circle of policemen who have surfaced behind him.

December hangs around the town, sombre and sulking as the police crowd around the bus with the sloganeers.

Kulay is only seventeen but his years do not stand in the way of severe punishment.

Ma decides to walk home from office that evening instead of taking the bus. Once she starts walking, however, she feels that her feet will just not stop. She walks past the mansion, and past the field, past the hospital and past several schools, past the posh localities, and then past the slums, past the library and past the church, past the little stream and then past the big one.

Soon she begins an ascent. On and on she climbs until she reaches the very top of Shillong peak.

In the confused orange light of the setting day, the upright stone monoliths look, to Ma, like a row of vicious hangmen who might stretch their arms and drag her on rollers up the steep, winding road and hang her once she reaches the peak.

She hurries on and when she reaches the summit, the obscure orange sky has translated itself into a slowly darkening night. She takes off her sari, folds it neatly and places it on a rounded bit of rock.

A perfect place to die, she thinks.

She stands in her petticoat, gazing at the foot of the summit from where she sees several streams gushing towards the empty buckets in town.

She is six thousand four hundred and forty seven feet above sea level when she realises that she has forgotten to fill her own buckets from the mansion's water tank on the sly.

It's too late now, she thinks wistfully, and starts walking back to town in her petticoat.

'Don't come near me, I farted.'

We stand outside the Class Eight door laughing at Kelsang.

'I ate one bottle of Hajmola and I farted.'

All the girls laugh at Kelsang's tales, which she narrates without smiling.

'I want to give birth to a zebra.' Kelsang clutches her stomach suddenly.

The girls are screeching now.

Moishree produces a fresh orange peel from her pocket and squeezes the juice from it onto my ruler. Then she holds the ruler to her palm and takes it away rhythmically making a web between my fingers.

'Chishhh,' Kelsang points at my skirt. 'Chishhh, there's a stain.'

'What stain?'

'Blood—blood—its blood,' Moishree dances in panic. 'Get to the infirmary for a sanitary P...'

'Why?'

'To put down there.'

I am warm, wet and red and I rush out frightened.

May be it's the zebra coming out of me after all.

I hide frightened in the toilet until the school bell rings and then rush panicking all the way home.

Ma returns late at night. Addy is horrified to see her staggering into the To-Let House in her petticoat.

But Ma behaves as if nothing has changed.

'We can't afford to buy sanitary pads.'

Ma rips off small strips from her old sari and hands them to me.

'Put them under there and wash them when they soak—ask Addy to tell you how.'

For ten whole days the thick alien blood trickles out of me in strange-smelling streamlets of growing-up.

At school I can't bear anyone next to me.

At lunch-time, I wander alone to the Monkey Jump where the big girls don't go anymore. The junior kids are screeching all around the playground. I sit and watch them for a while, praying for the blood to stop.

It is pitch dark in the crowded cell that Kulay has been led into. Through the stench, a voice gathers the courage to ask if there are only Khasi boys in the room. No one speaks for though they are all Khasis they cannot be sure who the other people are.

Eventually the dark eases. Kulay grows accustomed to the dim contours of the men and boys.

Someone offers him a lunch box filled with rice. He retches at the smell. He can now see the prisoners going in and out of the toilet, for there is no door to conceal them.

Perhaps he does not exist. Perhaps he has never existed.

It is almost midnight when the barred door swings open and a thin beam of light pierces his eyes. An Officer punts him awake.

As he kicks the criminal into the opposite room, the Officer is gratified at the thought that 'work is worship'.

He beats the boy until his own arms ache.

Kulay's mind is racing for a name he can call out each time he is dealt a blow. He has very little time for the Officer is soon replaced by a *hawaldar* who is drunk. He has enormous boots and unleashes a frenzy that has been bottled up since the day of the St. James demonstration.

Kulay tries hard to summon up a hatred of the *dkhars* but the taste of blood in his mouth weakens him and he lies there moaning in a pure pool of blood. He wishes they would shoot him. Hatred swells his veins but he lies there defeated and wonders why there is no one in the world he can think of as his own.

Clanking his tins, Governor arrives to whitewash the To-Let House again. This time on Redcoat's orders.

He brings a bright green ladder to reach the higher part of the walls.

'Where might the other slaves be?' he asks, angry at having to work alone.

It is Sunday.

He wears lens-less spectacles from which his bushy eyebrows make inquiries of the world.

'And how would you like being a big girl and walking back from school?'

Governor breathes fiercely through his emotional nostrils highlighted by his yellow jacket. He offers me his hand.

'It would be nice...'

I watch his boots right on the edge of the bright green ladder. Black boots with white snow. I ought to be shining them.

When he goes I pull out my own worn-out shoes. They are twisted and crunchy from all the pebbles that have got into the soles.

When I can look through the holes in the shoes I hear psalm singing and see Governor's coffin carried out and strewn with dead wreaths. Then I realise that the taxi-driver with the take-it-or-leave-it attitude is dead and I dance in revenge, for he is finally forsaken by all humankind.

> *Dance she did and dance she must,*
> *Even through the dark nights.*
> *The shoes bore her over thorns and briars,*
> *Till her limbs were torn and bleeding.*

'Wash your socks,' Sister Christine barks at morning prayers. 'Wash your socks and shine your shoes. I want to see my face in them.'

'I want to see my hairy face in them,' Kelsang mimics Sister Christine.

Everyone laughs at Kelsang's jokes. Everyone flocks around her. Kelsang's parents own the restaurant named after her and she gets pork noodles for lunch thrice a week. That's the day she draws the biggest crowd.

'I can tell you a way to see your future husband's face.'

Kelsang is sitting on the mossy steps that lead up to the statue of Virgin Mary in the stone cave behind the chapel.

'How?' Moishree asks wrinkling up her nose.

'Take a candle in one hand and an apple in the other. When the clock strikes twelve, walk backwards towards a mirror, with all your clothes off. Keep walking until you reach the mirror. Then look in the mirror.'

'Here, here, girlies.'

Sister Christine claps from the distant chapel window. She is reading the Bible with her magnifying glasses close to her eyes.

'Do you know Sister Christine is a man beneath her habit?'

Everyone runs down the mossy steps staggering with laughter. Sister Christine claps loudly behind us.

I try to smile against my will. Then without smiling Kelsang asks me, 'Why do you have such a long face?'

They all laugh again. But I know I am lovely like Phoebe and in the evening I will brush my long, silky hair.

Kulay lies in his own filth and pain craving for an impossible kind of strength that refuses to let his brothers die. His hatred returns in waves like a life force.

He sees his own body swinging from the nearest pole, unrestrained by a crucifix and unremembered by the people whose souls he has tried to save. Or perhaps they might give him an honorary title after the warrior who died fighting the British.

'What happiness to die for my country!'

The blood swims through his wounds. Consciousness comes and goes.

In these wakeful interludes, he thinks about fantastic escapes. His fingers are broken. He wonders deliriously if May will kiss them better when she sees him in this state.

At one searing moment, he almost surrenders. He knows things about the Union. He might trade these for a few minutes of relief. He feels like a rat, a mole screaming: 'Not me. Not me. Not me. Not me, but Martin, Terri, and Revise from up the lane.'

> I'm not a bus or a cat or a rat
> I'm a mole and I live in a hole.

Before Kulay's broken fingers have a chance to heal he is out of jail. He has no idea he owes this sudden liberation to May's intervention. Nor does she wish him to have any idea of her singular good deed.

May got wind of Kulay's arrest only in the New Year. She had hoped to spend more time with Benji but he was too preoccupied. In retaliation, she started going to posh parties again. It was at one such New Year's party that she first got a whiff of the boy's arrest. It was here again that she had used her evergreen charms with men of influence and lobbied for his release.

17. LETTERS, 1985

The Ides of March (Do you have J. Caesar for English?), 1985

Dearest Di,

Sorry. I don't think I'll be coming back to Little Rose Convent this year. In fact I'm almost beginning to feel settled in Class Nine, Bernard's school. You know its co-ed now. I can't help it. She (May) has begun to howl. I have to go by bus since May forbids me to cycle alone from here. Send your replies through Moishree who also uses this bus.

How is Kelsang? Write to me about drunken Debra. Is she still the Class Teacher?

We can meet in the lake. I miss school and all the morons. How is Redcoat?

Write and tell me EVERYTHING—don't leave out ANYTHING.

The milk has spilt (I did it) and my ink's running out. May is screaming.

So bye-bye!

Love,

Me (Who Else?)

April Fools Day, 1985.

Dearest Clemmie,

Nothing is the same after you left the school. Kelsang cracks stupid jokes and everyone laughs. I have no one to go to lunch with. I'm a rag in the wind.

Do you have any idea where Kulay has gone? I go to your house in the hope of seeing him but I don't!

Sister Christine called me today and told me to search each and every classroom for a dark green dustbin. She spoke in a low voice. Of course she always speaks in a low voice but it was unusually low today. So I went to hunt for the bin but I couldn't find it anywhere. After a while she came out of the chapel and said: 'I guessed it was you.' (I wonder why she said that). 'In which classroom did you find the bin?'

I told her I couldn't find the bin anywhere.

She said: 'Very interesting. Very, very interesting.'

If you were here we could have solved The Mystery of the Dark Green (Missing) Dustbin.

I don't know about Redcoat—she's mysterious.

Bye for now,

Di

April 27th, 1985

Dearest Di,

Did I mention that Benjamin is very scary and smokes a lot?

How is life in dear old school? Nice, I bet. It's horrible, HORRIBLE here. Nobody understands our kind of jokes. Trust May to act so smart. If only I had one wish I would wish myself back in Little Rose Convent again.

Please ask your Ma to shift you to Bernard's school. I can't go back because I've already got a T.C. (Transfer Certificate).

We are having sports and I have to do the march past. It's THE ABSOLUTE height of stupidity. I hate it. But I have to stay because of my problem parent (May—who damn else). It's like the Chinese way of torturing people before death by dropping water on their heads, drop by drop, till there is a big fat hole in it.

You'll never imagine how tough the studies are here. If I don't die this year of overwork and strain, I'll drown myself in the lake. I'm no brain box, which May thinks I am. I get headaches now because of the strain and you'll see me wearing specs like Addy next. Let's meet in the lake sometime. Any damn time. I'm desperate.

Sissy Kay has moved to the hostel. He's got a girlfriend and guess where they meet? In the green summer house by the lake. Do you know what he calls it? Sexy Point. Did you know it was called Sexy Point? I bet he made it up.

Please come home soon.

Clemmie.

May 10th, 1985

Dearest Di,

Guess who else is trying to look like a rock star? Revise—that snotty little boy who used to fly kites with Kulay... remember?

What is Kulay up to these days? He never calls up.

Revise plays basketball with us in the school court after school. But he never talks to us. Just grins. He's very shy. Slightly shorter than me.

We have to do a dumb drill with bamboo for sports day. It is very stupid. I hope May doesn't decide to turn up. Anyway, we're going to be the laughing stock of Shillong.

The girls here try to talk with an accent but fail miserably.

There's a Nepali girl in our class. She's not like Redcoat. She's nice fun.

I saw Kelsang wearing specs and walking to school. She was eating Hajmolas straight out of the bottle.

Please pray I don't fail. Form a prayer chain. Please send back a long letter through Moishree.

Clemmie

The Ides of June, 1985 (who cares)

YOU HAVE TO WRITE EVERYDAY. Please Di, otherwise I'll be dead from mugging. May is a tyrant. She locks me up in this windowless room and makes me study the whole day. I wonder what she does herself. She says I can't even write to you because you are still tenants in that house and neighbours of Governor. I don't understand them. I don't care whose neighbour you are.

You didn't say yes or no about going to meet Benjamin. Some girls who go to him are nice. But for the others I couldn't be bothered to mention them in my precious letter. (HAH!)

Did you watch the feature film on Sunday? Neelam looked damn cute but Govinda's pants were so tight, he looked so moronic.

We are allowed to bring comics and read them in front of the teacher's nose and they don't say anything. But I still miss Little Rose Convent.

I don't have any funny incidents to relate for the simple reason that none have occurred.

You are a FLOCCINOCINIHILIPILIFICATION. THAT MEANS WORTHLESS.

Solar systems of love,

Clemmie

July 4th, 1985

Dearest Di,

You know Revise smokes!!!

Anyway, May drops me at the Bernard's gate in the evening and I have to walk up the deserted driveway. It's damn scary since the girls say Father Geffen's ghost can be seen in the trees. You know he was the first principal of the school.

Guess what? Moishree comes to Benjamin for extra help in the evenings too (sickening) and she fell for one of the guys! He is just like Jughead —loves food and hates girls... any girl. Benjamin says he noticed how Moishree flashes her brilliant smile at him. I'm so ashamed of her.

Di, try to come to the lake and then we can go and meet Benjamin. I want you to meet him.

There's no discipline in our school. You can read Archies in front of the teachers and they don't say a WORD.

Benjamin says he knew it. He knew I would hate Bernard's.

Write a long letter before the holidays, ok? Write a long letter in small writing so that a lot fits.

Bye for now,

Clemmie the Great

August 5th, 1985

Dearest Clemmie,

The only piece of news I have is that Kelsang works in Sunset Bar and I can't be too sure if that is true either. There was a big rumour in class because there was one camp that said Kelsang had stopped coming because she was p... They supported it by the fact that Kelsang had turned up in a maternity dress for Colours Day. But the other camp said they had seen her walking past Momo Dome in a short mini skirt.

Either way, she's not coming to school anymore. That's all I have to tell you.

I have to learn Theorem 1-39. So bye.

Di

August 30th, 1985

Dearest Di,

I saw you from my school bus the other day coming out of the lake. In fact, I've seen you many times but it always happens that you're on the other side of the road or the bus is going too fast or something like that.

My arms ache from writing too much. I still hate Bernard's. (As if you didn't know.)

Remember, I told you about Revise? Anyway, he's damn irritating. He just stares at me. So we were all in Benjamin's room waiting for him to come and they were talking about this picnic. So I just asked Moishree who all were going.

I said, 'Just tell me who is going.' I just wanted to know.

So the next day she comes and tells me that she told Revise to come for the picnic because I had called him. It's unfair. I don't even know him that well. God knows what he'll be thinking. That I'm cheap and a flirt and he'll tell his friends.

What will I do? Trust Moishree to act so smart. I feel like slapping her stupid face. I don't even know Revise that well and she had to go and tell him that I'm calling him to a picnic that I'm not even going to myself. It was damn mean of her to insult me. It's going to spread and I'll have to get *badnaam*.

What can you expect from Moishree? Please pray I don't get *badnaam*. God answers chain prayers.

My whole life could be spoilt because they'll say: 'THAT girl... she called a boy for a picnic.' And what if May finds out? I think I'll go away from here to study somewhere else. Because here, wherever I go they'll point and say, 'THAT girl...'

Please pray for me.

Clemmie

September 7th, 1985

Di,

Tell Kelsang thanks for letting me know that Revise likes me. I find it too funny. Has Revise seen his face in the mirror? That day I was reading a TinTin in Benjamin's room while waiting for him to come and Revise was there too.

He's so moronic, I stare mockingly at him every time I see him. He's fit to be in a zoo.

I think you have grown a little fatter since the last time I saw you. Keep it up. How is Redcoat? You never tell me. Has Kelsang really left?

Guess what? I fought with Benjamin. He's very irritating. Doesn't let us laugh. Hate those brain box girls of my own age at Benjamin's. All they talk about is Benjamin. SICKENING!

Clemmie

September 17th, 1985

Dearest Di,

Tell Kelsang to tell Revise that I don't like him. Anyway, what stuff are you into these days? I'm damn scared but I won't let it show.

I saw Kelsang today again. She was driving a Maruti. I was inside the school bus. Kelsang was looking weird with huge sunglasses.

I've almost forgotten how to laugh and I have dark circles around my eyes.

Thanks for the long letter you sent me. It was so long that I could hardly read it. It took me two full hours to read it. (A matter of seconds, actually) Please write a long letter on Monday. Five pages or more – don't count both sides – small writing.

Please come to the lake on Sunday. I'll wait for you. Why don't you come or write?

My arms are aching writing such long letters to you. It's your arm's turn to ache, okay? Just your letter – long one – makes me happy, no matter what it's composed of.

I've got lots of sums Benjamin's given me to finish. I've got to buy violet kite paper and I don't know where to get it. No shop has that colour.

Write a long letter though I doubt I'll have time to read it.

Love,

Clemmie

October 30th, 1985

Dearest Di,

Damn mean of you to be going to Kelsang's shop without telling me. I see you coming out of the lake from the bus almost every day. How come Kelsang's parents allow her to run the bar? You must tell me all such things, okay? Don't forget.

Ok, Revise has stopped acting smart. I can't be bothered to *phasao* myself in such *jhamelas*.

Kulay has not come to church for ages. The other day I was telling Benjamin about Kulay and he said: 'Kulay who?' (Do you know the Knock-Knock Jokes?)

Did you feel the earthquake on Sunday? I didn't. (Surprising.)

Guess what? I was going down the path to Benjamin's villa and I was really late so I started running and I fell down. He saw me but it was damn decent of him not to laugh. But I flushed and blushed all the same. Anyway, when I finished tuition and we were coming out he fell down on the same spot. I was so happy because I was too embarrassed to face him but now it's fair and square.

Have you seen the Treetop ad? It's one of the few good things in life.

What are you doing for History? Culture or British Period or what? Who teaches you?

Love,

Clemmie

December 10th, 1985

Please do me a favour, Clemmie. Tell me honestly – I repeat, honestly – how feminine do you think I am?

On the scale below how would you rate me? Please I want an extremely honest answer.

1   2   3   4   5   6   7   8   9   10

Extremely Feminine   Extremely Unfeminine

Just tell me the number at which you would put me, okay? I've got my reasons for wanting to know, so just tell me, okay?

Oceans of love,

Di

December 15th, 1985

WHY ON GOD'S EARTH DON'T YOU LOOK AT MY DARNED BUS?

I screamed myself hoarse yesterday trying to get you to look, but fat chance. What do you think of so deeply? Everyone else saw me screaming and waving but you...

I didn't very well understand what you were trying to get at in your last letter. You seemed angry and hot and weren't able to write clearly.

Benjamin calls May a bulldozer to her face—she keeps ringing him up to ask him how I am doing.

I'm avoiding him since I flunked, as you know. It was so highly embarrassing. My *izzat* went through the earth and came out in Australia.

I have to mug now. I've spent nearly one hour of my precious time composing this piece of junk to you.

Let us try to meet during the holidays.

PS: How many subjects have you failed in? I failed in Maths - 17% and Khasi - 37%. Of course, I was expecting a big fat zero.

Let's meet over the winter holidays, okay? This year has gone so fast.

Clemmie

18. LAKE LOVE

When he returns to the mansion in the spring of 1986, Kulay is struck by the existence of a world that has revolved independently of his. It is materially comfortable. It has taste and fragrance. The concerns of its citizens eschew the searing physical pain that has focused his mind to a pinpoint during the lockup days.

The boy, who is now left largely to himself in the mansion, wanders through the sonorous house, seeking out the darkest corner to sleep in.

One day, quite by accident, he chances upon the library May had once zealously protected from intruders. He opens the door with reverence. Dust rises to meet him. Its once highly polished shelves are grimy and cold.

Kulay is caught between an eternal hunger and an eternal regret. He knows he must hide here. At night he sleeps on the creaking floor, beside the icy grate, for his sore body cannot stomach the surreal softness of the four-poster bed.

It is funny at first. I peep through the gate in the wall that separates us from the mansion expecting to see Clemmie, almost calling out, 'Clemmie, Clemmie, I'm coming to your house,' and no one answers.

Then I remember but slip through the gate anyway because Addy is away at tuition and Ma comes back only at five p.m.

I know that once Ma returns she will hector me to be more like Addy. Addy does all the housework, reads her story books from cover to cover yet always comes first in class. She has grown into a thin, silent girl with two thick braids and serious spectacles. She does not say much to me these days but she is not unkind.

But then, I am more interested in Phoebe now.

I've shined my school shoes a hundred times over and stood talking to myself in the mirror trying to be like Phoebe. I have tried hard to make her up. I have stood in front of the mirror stretching my words a little —not too much... just a bit... just like Phoebe.

Still, no one's home so I'm going across and I don't care what happens and neither do my knuckles as they bend into a knock at the mansion door.

Kulay opens the door and peers at a girl he only vaguely remembers. He is no longer inclined to bully and has grown increasingly melancholic.

He peers at the girl with the aquiline face and sharply cut hair remembering that he has shared something with her some distant time ago. It is a memory, an image and, despite the years he has been away, he knows exactly what it is.

Still he does not speak. The girl watches the boy but the boy remains perfectly still, stiff and cold.

I now know that Sister Christine doesn't really care about whether shoes are shiny or not. I polish mine bright black and she doesn't care to notice. Nor does anyone else, though my hands ache from shining my shoes and I take time off from my studies to make them extra brilliant. Then I go down on my knees and I drag out Addy's and Ma's shoes and sit shining them until they come back home, which is when I can go and wash my hands. But not before that and never alone, because of the arms in the bucket and the arms in the tap and the arms through the window, because of the many, many arms coming at me... slowly dancing.

'I'm watching a movie,' Kulay opens the door cautiously the next time I visit the mansion in the hope that Clemmie has given him a letter for me when she met him in church on Sunday.

He is wearing his brown leather jacket with the collars upturned. I take a deep breath as I enter the door, which he holds ajar for me. I can smell the aftershave on his skin.

I enter what used to be May's bedroom. There is very little trace of May except for the bed and the television.

I sit stiffly on one end of the stiff cane sofa and Kulay sits at the other end. It's a Russian movie and the subtitles go too fast for me to read.

Kulay speaks only when spoken to.

'Did Clemmie send anything for me?' I ask clearing my throat.

'Ya.'

He gets up and tries to take out the letter from his pants, which are far too tight for his hands to fit. I look away.

On the screen, the Russian actress stares in contempt at the boots of a stranger who is sharing her train compartment 'You hate men with dirty boots,' the man says, looking over his newspaper.

'She gave it yesterday but I forgot to give it to you,' Kulay sits down again.

'I'm going Kulay,' I get up after a while, though the movie hasn't finished.

'Okay.'

Kulay speaks inside his upturned collars.

I rush back wondering why I went at all. But the moment Ma lets me in, I wish I were back on the stiff sofa racking my brains for something to say to Kulay who, in keeping with his image, wouldn't say anything at all.

Crushed into his corner below the hanging portrait of Hilarious L, Kulay senses the sound of Redcoat's bare feet as they move surreptitiously in and out of the mansion. If he knows something is amiss, he does not say so.

News of the fresh agitation reaches him every day yet he does not feel strong enough to participate in it just yet. Quit notices have been served to illegal immigrants in several areas of the town.

In the mansion, however, Redcoat continues to preside over things as Governor rapidly degenerates and relinquishes the control he had never had. May continues to extract her rent though she never visits the mansion.

Kulay thinks about Di. The girl distracts him.

The next time I meet Kulay, Addy is with me. She is eager to play table tennis on the dilapidated TT table that has appeared in the garage. I follow her reluctantly. The insides of the garage are bare except for the murky green table. A tube light flickers from the ceiling. Governor has sold the taxi and lies about drunkenly all day.

Kulay doesn't smile. He is concentrating on the ball, hoping he can synchronise the movement of his wrist and his hurting fingers. He sends the ball smashing into the net. A sharp pain shoots down his arm and makes him curse so loudly the empty garage echoes with his voice.

From my side of the table, which is opposite the open garage door, I can see Redcoat drying her hair in the sun. Addy waits on the side patiently reading until her turn.

It is Sunday.

'You want to come for a fire in the evening?'

'You're doing a fire?'

'Ya.'

Addy blinks but doesn't say anything.

'If Ma lets...'

'Why do you have to ask? We're grown-ups now.'

Kulay sits feeding the fire with wood shavings. The orange glow lights up his face but his expression remains stony.

From the depths of the house, Di can hear Governor slithering on his green guitar. He is thinking of the rains in his village. He has not been there for a long time. He has submitted himself to Redcoat who is idly wondering if she can get a clan created in her name. She knows it is done sometimes when a *dkhar* woman marries a Khasi man. She wonders if she can persuade Governor to marry her.

Governor shudders at the grotesque faces he imagines he can see through the window.

The fire leaps up and throws shadows on the mansion.

He hears the rainwater collected in the bowels of the house gurgling in mirth at his plight.

He puts on his velvet trousers, his poor patched coat and his broad-brimmed cowboy hat and walks to the window in imagined grandeur.

He tries to catch his son's eye but Kulay looks away. They have not spoken to each other ever since Kulay returned.

We sit until the fire dies out and then walk back through the gate and shut the door.

Kulay kicks angrily at the antique junk that May had stuffed into the library when she vacated it. The room is not large enough for him to pace up and down. The shelves are stacked with the most incongruous literature through which Kulay hopes to wade, for he is slowly recovering his strength and is eager to soon emerge not only as a fiery leader of the people but also a fiercely well read one.

There is a tiny window at the far end of the library and he peers through the decaying lace curtains to see if he can spot the strange next-door girl once again. Though she does not know it, he had watched her intently as she sat opposite him warming her hands by the fire that night.

Her lips are dead.

Her face is coated with time.

He wants to wake up her mouth and taste the stories of what they did when they were little children. She must remember the games they played, the blazing make-belief world they had lived in, where he had lorded over the skies, and she had submerged into the earth.

Above all, she has no connection with the Union. She has spent no time attending demonstrations, distributing pamphlets, doing work in the villages, hoisting banners or burning flags. She does not know the implications of statements like, 'the police are on a beating spree.'

She does not know what it means to belong to a people or a place.

He knows she can never rebel, only elude. And now, though he knows it is insane, he longs to inhabit her secret world whose rhythms she has constructed of her own free will.

Ma comes home only at five p.m. Addy and I squat on the kitchen floor and make dinner. Addy is terribly serious because she has her High School Leaving Exam at the end of the year. She puts her books on a stool next to her and glances into them occasionally. She is huddled inside her responsible shawl and whispers as she reads. She is unmindful of how strange she looks. It does not seem to matter to her.

A faint knock startles us.

'Go and see who's come.'

I get up with pins and needles tickling my toes and rush to the door.

It is Kulay standing with his hands inside his jacket.

'Clemmie sent another letter.'

He produces a crumpled chit of paper and enters, even though I don't ask him.

When I open the note there is nothing written inside.

'I don't know...she sent it...'

He stares blankly as if he couldn't care less.

We stand awkwardly in silence. He stares hard at my face.

So I say, 'what?'

Kulay looks away and settles down on the trunk. He fiddles with the old cassette player. Music fills the room.

I keep standing. I wonder what he wants. The cassette comes to a screeching stop. I open the player and try to disentangle the tape. It is caught inside and chewed up. I try to pull it out slowly.

Kulay gets up and tries to help me. I do not push away his cool hands on mine.

'Come to the lake... Sunday.'

He lets go of the entangled tape and charges out.

I go back to the kitchen wondering why Kulay has asked me to the lake. Addy has put a pot of lentils on the stove and sits stirring it, with her nose still in her book. She does not ask me who it was.

I wonder what I'll wear when I go to meet Kulay.

It's so tough to have to conjure up Phoebe all the time when she's just disappeared into thin air. It's tough trying to look just like Phoebe. Kelsang says with better skin I might be close to pretty but that's not enough.

I've tried my best to get clothes similar to Phoebe's. The shades are beginning to resemble somewhat.

I shut the bathroom door and look hard at myself in the cracking mirror, wondering why Kulay asked me to the lake, until Addy bangs on the shut door and brings me back.

When I go to meet Kulay, the hawkers have got to the lake before me even though I am fairly early.

I walk awkwardly to the grassy slopes ignoring them. Water from the lake gurgles through a snaking pipe attached to a bright red fire engine. I think I see Borthakur out of the corner of my eye but I don't look. The whole area seems much smaller to me or perhaps I have just grown bigger.

'Didi, joota palishh?'

I look down startled at the voice that has called. I am surprised to see it is a woman in a tattered sari squatting before her grimy shoeshine box. It is a face I have seen before but stare hard as I do, I can't remember where.

I walk towards a speck on the slope that looks more and more like Kulay as I get near.

But it is the sight of the woman that is still with me. I haven't seen a shoeshine woman before.

'Did you have a good life when you died... good enough to base a movie on....?'

'What's that?'

'Jim Morrison.'

The lake is throwing up reflections of the weeping willow trees and the dainty boats are full of tourists.

Kulay no longer derisively calls them *dkhars* nor, for that matter, does he notice them.

'Your friend works in Sunset Bar.'

Kulay motions towards a tin shed painted green.

'Which friend?'

'Kelsang.'

'How do you know?'

'I go there everyday.'

'Why?'

'To drink... do you want to go?'

'No.'

Then he tells me that he knows about what Governor has done to me. I can't remember how he tells me. Somehow.

I clench my teeth and flop down on the grass.

'But that's your problem.'

We sit in silence.

I stare across at the shoeshine woman. It is getting darker and colder. She pulls her tattered sari around herself.

'Look there's the naked woman.' Kulay suppresses an embarrassed smile and points at the shoeshine woman. I remember who she is then. The naked woman, who once shocked Addy, Clemmie and I into silence.

Kulay races down to the renovated shop of the Bihari Brothers and, showing his fist, grabs a handful of sweets.

When the church bells strike seven, the two facing doors of the mansion and the To-Let House open like the cover of a fairytale and shut simultaneously. A shadow comes towards me. He takes my hand and leads me back inside the cover of his book. He shuts the toilet door and closes the lid of the WC. I sit down. He leans on the washbasin.

'Do you want some sweets?'

He feels inside his tight pant pockets and gives me a handful of toffees. I try to open one. It slips from my clumsy fingers through the crack in the toilet lid.

'I can't flush now,' Kulay whispers, dying of laughter.

'They'll wonder who shits Kisme sweets.'

'Kiss me.'

'No.'

'Yes.'

'No.'

'Not on my cheek... in my mouth. Eat it... slowly.'

It tastes of *kwai*.

Then, somewhere in the middle of the fumbling darkness, his hand hits the flush and sends me flying back through the gate leaving my mouth and its memory behind.

Ma comes back from work looking harassed.

'Don't mix up with Kulay... he's bad company,' she says, turning to me.

I keep silent and look at Ma. I've promised to meet Kulay in the lake again.

Ma picks up the sweater she is knitting for Addy and turns the wool around her forefinger.

Addy looks at me oddly but I keep silent thinking of my promise to Kulay.

Though Ma scolds and threatens me for a full week, she cannot prevent me from meeting Kulay. To spite her, I decide to accompany him to

Sunset Bar. Or perhaps this is because I cannot say no to Kulay.

When I approach the lake the next time, the shoeshine woman sits shrivelled up at the entrance but does not call out to me. I do not enter the lake but stand outside its broken fence waiting for Kulay. I am happy to be here. I am happy Kulay thinks that Governor is my problem. I don't need to think about it now. Just walk arm in arm with Kulay, no longer awkward like the first time, and enter Sunset Bar where I sit and watch him sip his golden liquor, some days with Revise and some days alone, and I feel hard and numb and reckless.

Revise sticks to Kulay even though he has long left the Union and is trying to be respectable. Kulay does not ask him any questions.

But the shrivelled woman troubles me. She sits gawking, as if she knows about my secret obsession. As if she is telling me, 'look what happens to people with obsessions.'

What if I was her? What if I spent nights writhing on the pavements soaked with winter and sat up shivering by an icy fire as the cold crept into my heart?

And still Kulay hasn't come.

A drunkard staggers towards me. But he doesn't look at me. Maybe I am not there at all. Cars pass by showing me up in their windows for a second. I try to stand in the sunny patch. I look prettier in the sunny patch. My hair is silken... my skin is white.

Solitary girl whose lips are curled... aren't you going to cry... aren't you?

The traffic policeman has gone home and the office-goers too.

And still Kulay hasn't come.

Now the mist is coming up and my loneliness is filling out into great big clouds in the sky. Any moment, something will shatter. Scurrying people open their umbrellas as the first drops of rain fall. Lightning races down purple in the face. No one looks at me. I try to blink away the raindrops from my eyes. My loneliness is moving upwards from my feet and soon it will grip my throat.

A schoolboy comes so near as if he wanted to trip on my outstretched legs. He turns back to look at me. Surely I am gorgeous like Phoebe. Surely.

But the loneliness is moving up fast now. It is already in my hands and I cannot open my bag to pull out my mirror. Now it's in my throat. I must press my cracked lips together. But I cannot breathe like that. So I try to take in a little breath and out jumps the loneliness. Out it jumps in freedom dancing. All the people stop to look at the strange, sad girl who has thrown up her loneliness.

And still Kulay hasn't come.

'Where were you,' they ask me when I get home. 'Where, where were you?'

Kelsang hustles Di into the cramped room at the back of the bar. It has a full-length mirror with clothes hanging around it making it look like a scarecrow. In front of the insolent mirror, under a photograph of Mr. Rinzen, Kelsang's father, shaking hands with the Dalai Lama, Di slips out of her uniform and into the jeans and sweater she carries in her school bag.

'Everyday, I look into this mirror and tell myself I'm gorgeous,' Kelsang says, as I am pulling my shirt over my head. She doesn't seem to care that I'm only half-dressed.

'And I'm laughing as I say it but I have to because no one's going to tell you that.'

She folds a pair of jeans thrown carelessly on the bed. Sunlight enters the room through the window covered with newspapers to keep out prying eyes. With the sun against her hair Kelsang looks like the haloed heroine the girls adored at school. Except, she no longer has her black mane but short cropped hair and a stupid little wispy pigtail hanging in front of her shrewd eyes that squint at everyone entering her shop.

I push back the brown faded curtain that separates the room from the shop and sit on one of the benches haphazardly painted blue and red.

Kulay swaggers in after a while followed by Revise who avoids my eyes because he suspects that Clemmie has told me about his interest in her.

'Hey Kelsang, he looks like John Travolta.'

Revise puts on an American accent and thumps the man who works rhythmically, handing out cups of tea and taking dishes away.

Travolta has an iron bracelet wrapped around his forearm.

'You can have Tibetan tea at my expense. Everything else has a price.'

Kelsang opens a large flask and pours out three cups of butter and salt Tibetan tea. It tastes like soup.

Kulay fishes into the woven red bag he bullied Revise into giving him, and takes out his Blue Book of Poems, which is nothing but an old daily engagement diary. He is not drunk enough. He begins to read aloud.

'*Every morning I wake up/ I say to myself, 'I love my parents'/ Every afternoon while having lunch/I say to myself, 'I love my family'/ Every evening at supper/ I say to myself, 'I love my family'/ But why the hell is it/ I don't believe it/ Maybe a change of perspective would help: 'I love you Governor'/ 'I love you May'/ And now I wish/ I could say that aloud.'*

Nobody speaks, expecting more to follow. I sit huddled over my cup of salty tea.

'*After having read a poem/ About a beautiful woman/ I turned around/ And saw a pair of boots on the floor/ What if I had read/ About a pair of boots/ And on turning around/ Seen a beautiful woman.'*

Kelsang has opted out of school herself, and encourages Di to do so too. Addy is immersed in her exams and no one knows Di is skipping three days of school every second week, except the teachers, and she doesn't care about them, just as they have given up on her.

Kulay is looking for something more. The walls of the mansion, which had turned into gold at May's touch, are now yellow and cracking. The old cabinets have dry rot. Kulay wanders here and there bumping into the furniture that seems to be coming alive. He tries poetry, he tries grass. As he gets more desperate, he goes on a permanent liquid diet of alcohol.

Di accompanies him on some of these journeys but there are no arrivals. Only a sense, on waking up, that they have to change—they must change. But no one shows them where to go, except Kelsang who stands at the door of the bright green tin shed and says: 'Quick! It's getting full.'

But when we sit on the grassy slope rising from the lake, Kulay refuses to meet my eye.

'Do you find me beautiful?'

'Yes, you're quite lovely.'

'Like Princess Diana?'

'Somewhat.'

'But it's Clemmie who's going to be a princess. In Benji's play.'

'Tell Clemmie I hate that Benji of hers.'

'Did you send him your poems?'

'On Jim Morrison.'

'So what did Benji say?'

'He said, "I have a beard and I might choose to write a poem on it." Then he said "Don't insult a dustbin".'

'It's quite funny.'

'I hate that prick.'

'Don't use those words.'

I can do anything/ I am the lizard king.

I meet Kulay at the gate of Ward's Lake on Sunday and tell him I'm still wondering about doing grass.

'How long will you wonder?'

'I don't know.'

'Anyway, you're too good to be true...'

I wonder what he means by that.

'You're a hypocrite,' Kulay says.

I am dry-mouthed.

I flop on the single stone bench by the lake. Governor had taken a picture of us here long ago. It was early winter and the light had softened Kulay's face. His cruel mouth had melted in that early winter sun. Propped up against the bench, he was almost smiling. Revise was in the background, too, looking melancholy and cold in his crumpled winter jacket.

Kulay is holding a cigarette and sulking now.

'Why didn't you tell everyone what the Dog did to you? Why did you keep shut?'

I look at Revise.

'Asshole,' Kulay spits out the words with the cigarette smoke. The sun hides behind the oncoming clouds.

Revise walks away.

I have nothing to say to Kulay, just as I had nothing to say to anyone. I stare blankly at him and feel the strength running out of my legs.

Then I remember Governor as I last saw him, and I know that the bad things catch up with you one day.

'I got her from the moneylender...'

Governor creeps up behind Kulay who has ventured into the drawing room and is gazing at a picture of May. Gooseflesh tingles on the back of the boy's neck and he recoils.

'This lady I happened to know for many, many years,' says Governor, picking up the photo frame and placing it on the table. 'She's been dead for a hundred years now.'

May's youthful picture smiles back happily at Kulay from across the mantelpiece.

Kulay is frightened and rushes back into his corner of the house from where he hears Governor roaring in drunken despair.

He wonders how it all went so wrong. He thinks of the photograph, of May smiling back at him with limpid, kind eyes.

'You want to go to May's house?' Kulay appears one late Friday evening when it is almost dark.

I rush to ask Addy, who is crouching under an orange tree watching a trail of ants. Addy has a wild look on her face and shrugs in response to my question.

Kulay has parked a scooter at the end of Solomon's Mines.

'It's Revise's scooter.'

The scooter refuses to start. The paint is peeling off at the spot where Kulay claims Revise banged a boy on the head with it. Soon we speed off. An autumnal chill pricks our skins.

I wonder whether I should hold Kulay to keep from falling as he speeds up the curving slopes, driving past the lake which is not yet lit up. He stops abruptly near a row of shops. May and Clemmie are waiting with huge shopping bags.

'Nee... Di is the good little girl she always was.' May tries to sound cheerful and hustles me into a parked car. Clemmie gets in.

'Park your scooter here, Kulay.'

The man at the wheel turns around. He is wearing green-tinted glasses.

'Why don't you write more often?' Clemmie whispers as the car starts. She is thinner and does not giggle that much.

The car has dark windows.

We drive in silence. The car pulls up at a large concrete house whose curtains are drawn. 'Why are there no lights?' the man asks May.

'I left my husband a few years ago.' May shuffles out with her huge bags.

Clemmie pushes me hurriedly into her room.

'At last.'

She flops down on the bed but Kulay barges in.

'Revise told me he likes you, Clemmie.'

Kulay is awkward and uncertain. He walks to her cassette rack and pulls out a cassette.

'Chisssh... Still listening to Wham... chish.'

'So what? Even Benji listens to Wham.'

'I hate Benji.'

I look around Clemmie's room. There are small stickers on the cupboard and posters on the walls. Kulay throws Clemmie's cassettes recklessly on the bed, destroying the look of the spick and span room.

'If you came to Benji he might give you something... he has lots of foreign stuff. Why don't you come?' Clemmie looks at me in her frustrated sulky way and her cheeks turn red.

'Let's go.' Kulay talks to me as if we belong to the same camp and are in enemy territory.

He walks out and I follow him glancing back at Clemmie, who is mouthing something I cannot decipher.

Kulay peers into May's ancient flowerpots where the flowers grow exactly as they wish.

May has disappointed him. The unvarying tang of her perfume that had driven him crazy with nostalgia in the mansion now simply reminds him of her constant need for attention. Clemmie has disappointed him by her absorption with her tutor and her extremely clean room.

He is stricken, perhaps for the first time in his life, by a terrible feeling of inferiority. He is certain Di will turn her back on him as soon as she recognises him for what he is.

He searches frantically in May's chest of drawers for something to entice her with when she comes to the mansion. In the lowest drawer, he finds some dried-up flowers.

'They must be a hundred years old,' he thinks, suddenly remembering something he had read in a book a long time ago. It was the story of an old man.

Perhaps *he* is the old man who has never been kissed. Like the old man in the story, he searches for the eyes that will look at him fondly. He searches for them in the chest of drawers. But all the while the silence inside him is singing. And it says that he can never have anything except his own funeral.

19. YOU TWO

'Where on God's earth did you find this elf?' asks Father Albert, Benjamin's friend and confidante, who is visiting the school mid year in 1986. He hands back a snapshot of Clemmie taken in the summer time when the villa was in flower and blooming.

It is noon as they saunter into the tennis court. The sun burns weakly.

'Once in a while, someone interests me.'

The snapshot snuggles back into the pocket of his white shorts.

'Is she your daughter?'

'No. But I'm terribly fond of her.'

'Too fond. Let her be. Put her out of the spot.'

The light returns to their faces from behind a passing cloud.

When Clemmie faces Benji on the balcony outside his room one day in the midst of a break between her sums, her memory takes a dynamic somersault and she remembers two things simultaneously.

She remembers the eye-crash where she had first seen Benji's eyes. She also remembers the afternoon when she had been learning Fur Elise with May.

It was quiet. Maybe Governor was out.

May had stopped playing abruptly. She had rushed out to the garage. When Clemmie followed her, she had seen Di slinking out of the garage quietly.

Is that why, thinks the frightened girl as she yields to Benji's reassuring arms, is that why my dearest friend in the world smiles strangely at times.

Benji watches her cautiously for she is there and yet not quite there. Still, Clemmie tries to remain the same sullen little siren, showing nothing of her discovery about the mysterious interconnectedness of things.

May awakes early one morning and finds her feet have turned to lead. She lies in bed helplessly staring at the plum coloured flowers on the crumpled bedcover wondering where she is. When she realises she is in her new home, she forces herself to get up. She has never been able to relax in the new settings.

She stumbles towards her burgundy clutchbag hanging inside her cupboard. She stares at the cupboard before opening it. The wood is far too new, too lacking in character.

Is she missing the smoke-darkened beams and lustrous wooden floors of the mansion?

'Certainly not', she snorts. She misses nothing. She yanks open the cupboard and pulls out her bag. But when she opens it, she becomes motionless again. There, in its crisp whiteness, sits a letter. There sits a loss.

She ties back her hair tightly and dons her *jainkersha*. She is going to sort out this house. Maybe she'll do some gardening. She has locked Clemmie in her room, hoping to force the girl to study, since five a.m. She stomps towards the modern gleaming kitchen. Then again the strange electric kettle arrests her steps.

Is her place only ever beside the smoky woodstove in the dark kitchen of the mansion?

'Certainly not,' she snorts.

All day long, she tries to immerse herself in this and that.

Ever so often something stops her. The secrets she carries in her heart knock at the door and demand to be entertained. She wonders why the pins of her conscience are pricking her flesh now when they have not done so in the past.

She feels the wisdom of her forty-three years weigh down upon her. Every man she has been with has added to her disillusionment but this last man, this Benjamin, this blithe Benji, has betrayed her best.

He must be the worst of the lot for he is so completely what he is not, she thinks, still reeling from the shock of what she has learnt.

The secret swims in her blood and her mind turns maudlin. She stares in the mirror and a charitable, conscientious, carnal, considerate, cruel Christian witch stares back at her.

None of May's many selves, however, stand in the way of the fierce and passionate letter to Benji, which is sitting in her bag. She writes that she is leaving him before he leaves her for she no longer respects the vacillating victim he has made himself out to be. I might be cruel, she writes harshly, but you are a cruel coward. That, in her eyes, is the greater sin and she minces no words in calling it such.

Now that the letter is written and her passion spent she feels a little vacant. 'Ben...,' she feels on the verge of uttering self-pityingly. But her mind darts quickly out of such emotion and forces her to change the subject. 'Ben... Big Ben. Ben... Bend. A hundred bends in the road.'

Clemmie is feeling feverish. She has had very little sleep the previous day as May had woken her up at the crack of dawn. Soon she falls into a sound sleep at the oblong cinnamon coloured desk in the villa.

'Clemmie...,' Benji whispers, undecided whether to wake her up.

She sits up and mutters something about Di. He interrupts her.

The words sink back into her mind, below her consciousness.

He watches her dark head drift back into the crook of her arm. A bulge within her books catches his eye. His suspicious hand inches towards it. But Clemmie slaps down her paw on his trembling hands as he reaches for one of Revise's unsolicited missives peeking out of her Maths book. Her freckles fry in embarrassment. What demon is this in him that does not quell?

Pain creeps into her stinging hands as he digs his nails into them.

'You!' she hisses.

Pangs of guilt leap up like large shadows.

He points his pen at the thick teenage dream inside the letter. It is sealed tightly so that no one might wake its wishful slumber.

'What's *he* doing there?'

'You told him to study with me,' an ugly whimper retorts, trying to use Revise's advances to make Benji envious.

'Since when has *he* been doing *that*?'

'Off and on.'

'I didn't know anything about this.' And he is not happy.

Benji paces up and down his garden, puffing on his cigarette anxiously. He had merely hoped to use the boy to deflect attention from himself.

'Damn it,' he thinks for he cannot even ask Clemmie what she thinks he should do. Perhaps Father Albert was right. Perhaps he has made this whole thing up anyway. This whole thing about Clemmie being an ethereal creature blessed with good sense far beyond her years is complete bullshit. The object of his paternal and passionate desire, he realises, is nothing but an ordinary school girl, haughty, headstrong and unhappy.

May does not want to stop Clemmie from going to Benji immediately. That may lead him to think she is bitter now that he had finally got her letter.

But am I bitter? she wonders. Why is she dwelling on herself? Why is she mellowing? Why is she so immobile these days? Men had come and gone. But this last man, this Benji-man had really thrilled her. Then he too, like the rest, had revealed his baser nature.

'You, Benji, too,' says a tiny tear as it threatens to roll out of her wrinkling brown eye. 'You too.'

She thinks then of her library, her Shakespearean books, her life full of fury and silence.

No she will not return to the mansion just yet.

No she will not recall Clemmie from Benji's just yet.

No she will not cry quite just yet.

Ma cannot stop thinking about what it might feel like to be touched again. Everyday, as she walks to office, Han Chu stands outside his Chinese restaurant and whistles a tune from a Hindi film song. The unspoken words of the song leave a deep impact on her.

She is flattered.

To further her acquaintance with the oblique admirer she creeps into the chicken pen that stands on its clawed feet behind the tenant quarters and hastens to gather the chickens. As the office siren sounds in the air she rushes into the Chinese restaurant holding a fattened chicken in both hands.

Han Chu stops whistling as he surveys the fowl that the unhinged woman has let amok on the linoleum floor of his restaurant. He makes a good bargain for the live chicken which the woman offers him.

As for the flesh on the side that she seems to offer, Han Chu does not feel quite up to it. Some days later the woman reappears with more birds. Soon it becomes a normal affair for him to buy fowl from her at rates much lower than the market.

It takes Ma a while to realise that Han Chu is cheating her, caught up as she is in the illusion that he fancies her. When she comes to her senses she stumbles out of the restaurant, shouting obscenities at no one in particular. She raves all the way home and when she lets herself in to the To-Let House, she catches the eye of her younger daughter whose pained looks tell her how deeply in shambles their mutual lives are.

'You really did it?' Di can often look vapid. She is still smarting a little at being called a hypocrite but tries not to show it.

Kulay is confessing to his earlier acts of derision and violence though he does not describe them either as brave or cowardly, nor does he give her any details.

He is full of hate again. He feels, rising in his veins, the precise wave of emotion, or lack of it, that will soon enable him to burn police vehicles, assault immigrant grazers and torch their sheds with fanatic rapture.

'I just did it. I really believed... first... in...,' his face contorts.

Di finds it hard to love him in these lucid moments.

The wind nudges the tin roof of Kelsang's shed.

'Then... I was just doing things... I just don't like *dkhars*... like you don't like dirty shoes.'

I sit with him on the grassy slopes above the lake one lazy summer Sunday, as he lies scratching into his Blue Book. I sit beside him watching the stagnant green water.

Benji's heart winces a little as he faces Revise in the long dark study room of his house. He realises that he cannot hope to win against the young boy.

'What is Clemmie really like?'

Revise is surprised at his question. He chews his pencil. Then he looks around to see if the other students are in sight.

In the pause that ensues, Benji thinks of the last time he had seen Clemmie. She had, as always, looked troubled and enchanting. 'Yes,' he thinks somewhat dramatically, 'I will bury her in uniform.' Blue mohair blazer, pleated grey skirt, white knee-length socks and bright black shoes.

'You know her well don't you? Like her?'

A bird flies past the open window breaking into tune.

Man to boy.

From then on Benji makes it a point to throw them together. As if by accident. Slipping out himself.

Benji walks rapidly towards the village behind the villa. He has made this a habit. It helps him forget his jealously for a while.

The gravelled road that runs between the rice fields radiates before him in the last rays of the sun. It seems to map out his life ahead. He sees his skin wrinkled into longitudes and latitudes. He cannot turn back but must emerge an ancient man muttering, 'too old for you. Too old for too much.'

The land, rustic and green, curves to meet him as if in a flicker of recognition.

He looks up at the sky. The villagers are hostile. But he has to live here amongst them, in the middle of these tilled fields and tarred roofs. He has tried to be somebody in this town. And indeed, he is a man of importance. The rich and famous desire me, he thinks. He can have a million Mays if he so wishes, and perhaps a trillion Clemmies.

Two tallish twilight shadows appear around the bend startling him. They are the shadows of Revise and Kulay returning from a grassy field trip.

'It was his fault.' Kulay kicks Revise as he tells me how they had bumped into Benji.

They had taken a long walk together chancing upon places in Shillong they had never known existed, and had met Benji on their way back from one such excursion. He had cast a sidelong glance at the two boys, sniffing the alcohol on Kulay's breath.

'He told me I didn't smell anymore. That's how I went ahead, anyway.'

'What did Benji say to you?'

'He told me I was a dog fit to walk with my tail between my legs.'

We are standing inside the Plaza in the town centre. Kulay has come here to buy the long, smuggled cigarettes that are good for smoking grass. I am already high on my share.

Waves of shoppers drift towards me.

Suddenly I seem to lose the boys. I am tossed about and afloat. Then I spot them at the far end of the corridor. A large glass wall runs along the corridor, overlooking the street below. I walk along it, trying to catch up with them, but can't walk fast enough. It seems as if Kulay is taking a lunatic plunge through the wall. He crashes through the glass and hurtles to the street before my eyes. I open my mouth to scream. Shards of glass fill my throat. I scream out in spite of them, with agonising pain, even though I only imagine Kulay has crashed to the street.

The day is turning to dust.

Revise comes towards me moving vaguely.

'Where's Kulay?' I slur.

'Coming...'

Kulay appears and starts walking ahead with Revise.

'Chicks,' they look at each other and smile.

Kelsang crosses the street and walks over to where we are standing. She invites us to her shop. We refuse. She walks off into the dizzying traffic. In the distance a car whizzes past her.

'Hit her.' Kulay screeches.

He has become a black hole... falling under his own weight... disappearing into nothingness as he sucks in everything in his path and dissolves into darkness.

When Clemmie reaches the villa, Benji is polishing his shoes with a red toothbrush.

'I can do that for you.'

'No.'

Clemmie cannot remember how many days have gone by since she last came. In truth, it has only been a few long days in which something has inexplicably altered.

Perhaps it is Benji's eyes. They have moved out of the deadening debris of the eye-crash and begun to blink.

Blink. Blink. Wink.

Out blinks the human heart and in winks its heartless replica. In comes wisdom and weakness. Out goes the mad strength of definite connection.

'Benji...'

A sullen priest goes past his door.

'ALBERT...' He hops to the door wearing only one shoe.

'How can I get you out of my head?' Clemmie addresses his back. 'When I read a book, I feel you turning the pages. When I return home, I feel weightless and race to my room knowing you are watching me. It takes me so long to take out my maths book.'

Clemmie feels his voice in her hair and on her neck... and it is so different from anything that has ever happened to her before.

But the softness spreads itself thin and slips away. She clenches her teeth for she doesn't want to let him go.

When he comes back from conferring with Father Albert at the door, Clemmie does not face him.

'So how many sums did you get absolutely wrong?'

He is holding her by the shoulders.

'Be steady, Lady.'

She can smell the polish from the brush. She hasn't told him much.

If I ever get home from here I'll make a list of what I can take and what I absolutely can't, Clemmie thinks. She could eat shit, she says to herself, but she couldn't stand losing Benji.

'Sums, Clemmie. Sums, Sums, Sums...' He is still holding the toothbrush.

'Chish... you're brushing your teeth with that.'

'Yes,' he shows her his teeth. 'Don't you know its charcoal... good for big white teeth?'

Clemmie gets two sums right.

Suddenly, the lights go out. He goes on teaching as if nothing has happened.

It is only early evening but everything turns dark.

'I think Kulay is dead,' Clemmie says suddenly, shivering at the premonition.

'So am I. Forget about me, Clemmie. I'm dead.'

'Where's your voice coming from then?'

'From the bottom of the Dead Sea.'

'Have we drowned?'

Clemmie scrapes her chair to get up.

'Don't move. You'll bang into something.' He reaches out in the darkness and pushes open the door.

The evening light creeps in. He gets up slowly and stands at the threshold. Everything is quiet. Frozen. Cold stars are blinking blue. He is standing at the door—silent. Clemmie, still on her chair, forgets to breathe. If she moves, she will be back inside a room full of hard, bright numbers.

'All right.' The light comes back with him. '$a^2 + 2ab + b^2 = ...?$'

Kulay and I have kissed each other on the mouth seven times but on the eighth occasion, Kulay tells me that we could be shot if discovered.

This is not true, but by the look in his eyes, I know that he believes it to be so.

I ask Kulay if I need to take permission from the President of the Union before kissing him.

'Yes,' He is very serious.

The Union, relatively dormant since the riots, has woken up with a start and reiterated its demands. These are genuine demands and no one feels them more genuinely than Kulay.

And so the day the Union dips its fingers in black ink and reconfigures the writing on the wall, Kulay returns, once again prodigal and once again profound, from the girl's arms to the cold revolution he knows he is destined for. He is racked by an irrational guilt because of his association with the girl. He has quickly grown frightened of her... of himself with her.

What if they come to know of it in the Union?

There is no stated ban against associating with the *dkhars*... but entering their mouths, embracing their sins...?

He knows he can only absolve himself of his transgressions by returning to the Union.

A potent excitement, not anymore from love, but from a lucid desire for war torches up inside him.

'Kulay?'

But he does not answer.

'I know, so don't tell me.'

'I'm not.'

He cannot confront Di. He is sullen and clamps up every crevice in his body.

She cannot enter.

The stones roll into the mouths of his caves and they are now shut against her.

He is writing madly. Lying in the damp library, he writes on the cover of books, inside their pages, over their words, between their lines and in their margins.

The town, meanwhile, remains plunged in darkness for the Union has ordered black flags by day and black-outs by night. The city has split wide open and there are two sides again.

'If I live underwater/ for sometime and/I don't die/ I think I'll survive.'

Kulay utters the lines under his breath. We are walking towards the lake single file.

To win him back, I have promised to do grass with them again.

The grass grows wild and takes you places. Revise stores it in the pages of his notebooks. It spawns good poetry.

'Not just by being there,' Revise says. 'You have to take it, dry it and roll it in a cigarette or a pipe.'

It makes me laugh – and then cry – to think of Kulay sucking on his pipe.

We walk past an urchin-driven horse cart. Revise says he would like to spend his life sitting in the lake, doing portraits of people for only ten rupees.

A newspaper boy thrusts his papers towards us. We move away.

'What's the wildest thing you've done?' I try to keep pace with Kulay.

'Hit beer bottles on the mansion windows... not had a bath for two months.'

Kulay must always smile at Revise before he answers.

Kelsang's place is swarming with people today—students, lovers, dropouts. I feel out of place in the rush.

She is wearing a short denim skirt. She carries armloads of disposable cups and teabags.

'Don't get fooled with the spoons and the forks: 'THEY ARE NOT DISPOSABLE,' Kelsang winks at us. 'Travolta will have to fish them out of the dustbin if you dispose them.'

'She's married with a kid,' Revise tells us, when we sit down at the red and blue benches.

'Of course not.' I feel defensive about Kelsang.

'Shut up!' Kulay is rolling a cigarette. 'I'll read 'Wishes for my Mother' if you get a kick.'

Kelsang mimics Kulay. He turns red and gets up.

'Just joking, ya,' Kelsang says innocently, but Kulay has already kicked the bench and thrown a handful of spoons into the dustbin and walked out with Revise in tow.

'What are you doing for your pimples?'

Kelsang turns towards me as if nothing happened.

I hate her at that moment. And hate her again while she sits next to me and describes her morning beauty rituals, 'I force a spoonful of garlic with two glasses of lukewarm water down my throat everyday.'

She pulls me towards the back room.

'C'mon just try something. Just look in the mirror and repeat my lines.'

The aroma of steaming momos rises through the shed.

'You're the most beautiful woman in the world,' Kelsang addresses herself, 'You're fascinating...'

She applies a little more lipstick and purses her lips so that the garish pink spreads evenly.

I stick out my tongue and touch the cold glass. Saliva drips from the glass blurring my face. In the depths of the salivating mirror I see Travolta lurking outside the half open curtain. Kelsang grins satisfied.

But it's not enough. It's not enough. And when we emerge from the back room, I rush outside in search of Kulay and the harder stuff.

Kulay is sitting on the slope that rises sharply from the lake. The water is shimmering. You want to throw yourself into it. The grass is green and full of shit.

'I love dirt.'

Kulay throws himself on a sunny patch.

He plucks a blade of grass and chews it. He never looks directly at me —Kulay never does. Revise is looking far away too. I have smoked three cigarettes since I found them and am waiting for something to happen.

'I want that green fruit which you eat with red chillies.'

Revise races across to buy the shredded fruit sprinkled with salt and chilli flakes.

'I hate fruit...' Kulay chews ferociously on a blade of grass. 'I don't care,' he says. 'I don't really care... you take me too seriously... I'm never serious about anything.'

He is sitting slightly above me and I have to turn around uncomfortably to look at him.

'I wasn't going to come... I thought you were angry with me because I called you a hypocrite.'

'I was just... hurt.'

'But who cares...'

'You don't care because it hurts to care...'

'You're just like any other girl. Just like any other girl I know.'

Revise offers me some fruit. It tastes putrid. I offer it to Kulay. He chucks it.

'I was offering you some...'

'I thought you asked me to throw it.'

It is 1 p.m. Revise has dozed off.

I turn around to look at Kulay and imagine something hits me. It happens so fast. I hurtle with Kulay like an avalanche down the slope. For one crazy moment, we are suspended in the air then crash downwards breaking open the green still waters.

'Asshole,' Kulay kicks Revise. 'Let's take her home. She can't take it.'

I get up and rush towards the gate where the hawkers sit.

The shoeshine woman has washed her dirty silver hair in the lake and sits drying it in the sunless light.

It seems to me Kulay kicks her and she screams. Then I feel him shake me up.

'Why are you screaming? Stop it.' Revise shuts my mouth with his hands.

'Why did you kick her?'

'I told you girls can't take it.' Revise tries to wash my face in the dirty lake water.

'Let's go home,' I beg.

'I hate home... that's the place I avoid going to... that's the place I go to when I have nowhere to go...,' Kulay walks back to Kelsang's shed.

Di knows, as she sees him moving rapidly away from her, that he is no longer a part of her. She feels the ache in her phantom limb, not wanting to believe it has been severed from her. Tears trickle down her face as she remembers the long ago winter night when she had crawled back tremblingly into the four-poster bed, preceded by Addy and Clemmie, after May had had enough of the healing moonlight and was ready to charge back into the kitchen and go for Governor.

'Because he's not my son anyway,' she heard May screaming in the faraway kitchen, while Clemmie and Addy lay fast asleep. Or so she thought until she heard a slight, ever so slight whimper, and knew it was Clemmie's nose sniffing like that under the quilt because she had heard more than Di had.

'Mrs Potato,' she heard Clemmie pleading after a while, in troubled sleep. 'Mrs Potato, don't pull down Kulay's kite like that.'

But it was too late to plead because May was already holding his torn kite drunkenly in her hands.

Di draws out this weapon of a secret she has saved from a long time ago and marching into Sunset Bar, hurls it at Kulay as he sits on the blue-red bench staring into space.

'You are Redcoat's son.'

He does not try to stop her. They do not speak.

She looks at him directly. It is only a passing glance, full of contempt and disdain.

Kulay listens without his ears to what he always knew.

Revise listens too. Slowly his mouth turns in and inner still. Then it turns into a scornful sneer.

There is nothing more to say.

We sit awkwardly in silence.

It is cold.

Benji is on the verge of changing his mind. He will need all his strength to make a final break, to put a stop to Clemmie's visits. 'God,' he shivers in his weakness 'what kind of test is this?'

His thoughts shift indulgently to Clemmie. A fragile sapphire globule embedded in a skeletal silver ring had once glinted from her finger. He thinks of the ring crushed beneath his huge clumsy foot.

He looks out at the tender white flowers that have appeared on the dark branches of the tree outside the villa. The branches firmly uphold their floral charge even as they painstakingly stretch skywards. He thinks of the white mush that will ensue if the heavily branched tree turns against its white offspring and comes crashing down.

'How much more help do you think you'll need?' May is anxious to stop Clemmie's villa visits but tries not to show it. She walks to the tall French window framed daintily by thin rose-coloured lace curtains, wincing from the stab she imagines Benji has thrust into her back.

The ground outside the window has not yielded any flowers. She misses gazing at the flowers she had grown in the mansion, but then she knows that it isn't only the flowers.

It is also the dear old parlour window that had framed them and the hoary wicker chair that defied the weight of the years. She is transported back to the mansion and wonders what has become of Kulay. A vaguely maternal anxiety creeps into her heart, but she forces herself to harden up and think only of how she might avenge herself through the boy, should she ever meet him again.

20. RETRIBUTION

'You're not studying Di,' Ma startles me out of a letter I am writing to Clemmie.

I know from her tone that she is about to say, 'Look at Addy—can't you be more like her?'

'It's not my fault,' I want to shout back. It's not my fault I'm not like Addy. It's not my fault I'm not like Phoebe. It's not my fault Clemmie has gone away. It's not my fault I want to be alone in school. It's not my fault I go across to meet Kulay who is unkind to me now because he is smarting under the dark secret I have revealed to him. It's not my fault Ma works hard—as hard as two people.

I walk out insolently and slip through the gate into the mansion compound. The garage doors are open. Kulay is not in sight. I pick up the table tennis bat placed on the shelf in the garage and start bouncing the ball on it.

I'm reaching fifty one bounces without dropping the ball when I turn around and see Governor enter.

'I'm waiting for Kulay,' I stammer bravely 'I just want to play.'

Governor is wearing his boots, which are unzipped all the way down to the soles. He has been drinking all day.

'You know May left me...'

He staggers towards me, shutting the door behind him and snaps on the harsh tube light.

'And your friend, Clemmie, too. All left...left, right, lef...'

It is still light outside. Kulay slowly creaks open the door allowing a stream of light to enter. Governor is still holding me from the back as if he were teaching me to hold the bat properly. Kulay is still far away but he is coming nearer.

'Don't move too much,' Governor whispers harshly.

Kulay does not go away but stands there staring at us as if he knows but doesn't care anymore.

'Kulay!'

The silent garage echoes with Governor's voice.

He does not answer.

Governor is enraged by his silence and, in his anger, lets go of me. He charges outside. Kulay stares at Governor with bloodshot eyes.

I find my way to the door and run past Kulay, who is looking very far beyond me.

Han Chu's derision has temporarily jolted Ma out of the insanity she had begun to submit to. For once her thoughts turn to someone other than herself. She peeps through a crack in the wall that separates the To-Let House from the mansion and considers the spectacle of her ravaged daughter with something akin to sympathy. Is this child old enough to handle pain she herself has been unable to endure, the pain that has driven her out of his home, made her humiliate herself and forsake the strength she could have found within?

I rush out through the main gate of the mansion and out into the street. I can't go home just yet. Ma will wonder why I came rushing back and Addy will notice there is something wrong.

I slip into Solomon's Mines. Borthakur is sitting at the counter as Redcoat has stopped attending to the shop ever since she moved into the mansion. I find my way to the last grimy seat and sit in the shadows waiting.

'Hello Monika?' May's friend who is buying sweets from the counter startles me.

She has mistaken me for someone else. Will she realise it? Should I tell her I'm not Monika but someone else? How does it matter? I'm happy to be Monika. Monika is not the girl who has come out of the garage and nothing unusual has happened to her. Monika is just a girl. She is sitting at a table with her hair shining, and she is talking to May's friend. I want to be Monika or Phoebe or anyone but not me.

'When did you come back from Bombay?'

I don't know. I can't be Monika because I don't know when I came back from Bombay.

The game is up.

'I think you've mistaken me for someone else.'

I've been mistaken for someone else twice today. Once here in the shop for Monika, and once in the... garage... completely mistaken.

But she's remembered, 'Oh yes. But you look so much like Monika. Anyway, how are you?'

Then she's already going away. Even though she just asked me how I was. She's already moving. She's outside the door and onto the pavement, waiting to cross the road. But she did want to know how I was just now. And I was about to tell her. Or did she want to know how Monika was.

'I'm fine,' I call after her, because if I was Monika I would be just fine.

But she's already crossed the road.

Clemmie is wondering if she ought to write to Di, describing her state of mind. The fear of betrayal has begun to stalk her ever since the day Benji had asked her to forget about him saying he was dead.

'Di,' she begins, 'I'm just very sentimental about Benji. I fall into a routine immediately without questioning why I am doing this. What is the need? It must be so difficult. He doesn't have anyone to talk to. Or at least that's what I thought. I'm quite sentimental about these stupid things.

But does he think I am old enough to handle this?'

But then Clemmie stops writing. She lifts the crisp white sheet of paper and tears it into tiny little bits. She painstakingly splits each word on the paper into its letters and then mixes up the little bits into a small pile. Bringing out a lighter she has stolen from Benji's room, she sets the pile of paper on fire.

Governor has just lifted the lid of May's piano when Kulay enters the mansion. There is a reminiscence painted on the inside of the lid. It is the picture of a blue kite brought down by the drunken hands of a woman who is not his mother.

Kulay goes berserk. He shoves Governor out of his way and, with all the strength he can muster, pushes him out of the brass-knobbed door of the mansion. Then with staggering energy he hunts down Redcoat and, like a child cruelly dragging a rag doll along the floor, brings her to the door and kicks her out as well. Soon he is upturning the ancient flower pots that once grew carnations as they pleased, breaking the ornate armchairs and setting the cabinets on fire.

> *Out! Out! Get out!*
> *Out! Out! Get out!*
> *Out! Out! Get out of town!*

In late 1986, Shillong is burning over the issue of illegal immigrants. The latter have been hastily gathered in camps on the edge of town. Busloads of fleeing immigrants, on their way to the camps, are intercepted by groups of young boys guarding vantage points in many localities.

The town has lost all sleep.

Kulay scrounges the corners of the mansion for any object that might remind him of Redcoat. An unending ecstasy of utter recklessness has been gushing through him since the day before, when he helped reduce the Umro school building to ashes. He wants to burn down her smells, burn down the mansion where pungent weeds and green skeletons wildly clutch the decaying timber. He wants to torture her, to smash her into a hundred bits.

He lumps her belongings with those of Governor's and, slipping out of the mansion, slides them into the lake whose ripples appear to tremble with the beating of the drums.

He looks up from the water and knows that the boys have reached the relief camp where Governor must have taken refuge with Redcoat, whose status in the town has long been illegal. He lowers his head and stares at the rippling green lake. All he sees is the battered face of the boy who has betrayed the parents he never wanted.

He had always been aware of the *shi-piyas* in the Union, the half-breeds.

'It's not that we don't know we are mixed blood,' they would confide in him in moments of drunken intimacy. 'We know. We are aware of it. Because this cannot be really hidden... it's not a taboo, its acceptable... Even that great leader, that what's-his-name... was also bloody half blood...'

They would turn subtly aggressive. The problem was not that they had been kept in the dark about their origins. The problem was that they thought of themselves as blue-blooded Khasis.

This was the lie that crushed most of the *shi-piyas* in the Union.

And like them, Kulay now, was squarely faced with the choices that were not available to him.

He could not choose his parents.

Governor's presence in the refugee camps causes a commotion of which the man himself is oblivious. But the men, women and children are dirty and harassed and they do not wonder about his incongruous presence for long.

Some of them move into the basement of the five star hotel, which is still under construction, overlooking the Umiong river near the camp. But everyday more come in, herded into trucks and dumped in the camp.

It is dark in the entrails of the unborn hotel.

Soon Governor arises like a Messiah and, shrugging off his anonymity, announces, 'I'm going to the market.'

Candles.

Matches.

Rice.

Firewood.

Soap.

Tea leaves.

Sugar.

Salt.

When the Sisters of Mercy arrive, they stand watching the man who has never stepped inside a church, working enthusiastically to alleviate the misery of the downtrodden.

Governor is grateful to the Sisters of Mercy on this dismally divided day. A premonition of retribution creeps up his back, chilling the sweat from his redemptive labours.

It is dark when a jeep full of Union boys arrives at the camp that has been steadily swelling as more and more immigrants, fearing for their lives, slip beneath its tents and try to hide themselves. Curfew has been clamped on the town but the boys do not feel obliged to restrain themselves.

'You have to stop this..', a familiar voice makes Governor turn around.

'Ay?' He peers at Terri's face, wheezing heavily.

Terri gives the man a tentative prod, pushing him to the very edge of the still, green river that runs along the camp.

Governor fears he will soon be thrown into the icy cold water. He feels tired at the thought of the long swim ahead of him. If they shove him into the river he will fall backwards. He knows he is empty for it is often said in the villages that:

> The empty-handed walk backwards.

'You are undoing what we are trying to do.' Terri's voice is rough and disrespectful. Even so the boy hesitates to throw Governor into the water.

He is overpowered by Martin who comes up stealthily behind him and, with a huge yell, sends the man crashing into the emerald green river.

The boys hoot and jeer.

Governor feels his death breaking through the green slime and wafting up towards him. He knows he is dying. Yet he also knows he is condemned to carry this knowledge of his end for a long time before he can finally rest in peace.

As the Sisters of Mercy help him out of the cold water, he finds his legs give way under the immense weight of his invisible cross.

Redcoat leaves the town with a busload of people who are returning to villages in their country where electric lights have not yet reached and most of their lives are spent in unyielding fields.

She suffers several kinds of pangs but none of them for Kulay, who had never been hers but an alien, seeking temporary shelter in her body until the time of its birth. And when it was born, crouching out of the foreign flesh, turning her blood to water, she had traded it as easy labour to keep the mansion fires burning.

May had been compensated by Kulay's life and labour. She had demanded it as soon as she learnt that Recoat was with Governor's child. It was none other than the loyal Borthakur, then a young mercenary working alternately for Governor and May, who told her of Governor's betrayal. As soon as the informer disappeared to spend the money she had rewarded him with on a good deal of opium, May sent for Redcoat and waited at the window of her library watching the woman arrive.

She made her an offer, which Redcoat, having nowhere to go, had fatalistically accepted.

May demanded her pound of flesh.

Redcoat sucked in her lips.

'Not my son,' she seemed to say.

'Never your son,' said May's calculating stare, for she hoped to punish the woman for her sin by demanding that her child be enslaved in the mansion forever.

A few months later, just as it was getting dark, a bundle was delivered through the kitchen door of the mansion. Someone had laughed a witch's laugh. Someone had begun to dispense on the boy the poetic justice she still believed the world capable of.

No one had ever wanted him. How could May?

Yet she could not despise him. Though she had tried many times, she had never succeeded in making him cry. Her high heels had tried to crush his toys. Her hands had crumpled his kites. But the boy had fought back a determined fight against tears.

She knew that she had failed when Clemmie stayed up one warm summer night keeping vigil beside Kulay, as he lay sweating from a particularly high fever and when Clemmie had given him her red polo-neck sweater to keep out his shivers, she had undone everything May had done to punish his parents by punishing him.

How strange he was, how uncomfortable in his school uniform, how suspiciously he regarded the tenants, how he convulsed in his dreams.

May's memory, being what it is these days, goes back further than she usually allows it to. She sees Kulay crouching beneath her bed, his grey eyes gleaming in the dark like a cat's. He gives her a terrible scare as she kneels down to pull out her sandals from under the bed.

No. She had not foreseen then that she might grow to love the golden boy, in ways neither menial nor maternal.

And now when she recalls his grey, stony eyes pelting her heart, she thinks it is her heart's fault that it beats for the underling.

'Me first,' Clemmie says, when I finally meet her near the lake a month after the agitation. We have been trying to study for the final Class ten exams which will be held after the winter break in March, 1987.

'Me first. That guy sleeping up there... don't look now...'

But I've already turned my head in the direction she's pointed. The man has covered his face with a newspaper. He is wearing a tattered school boy's sweater and torn pants.

'He just showed me a knife and said *yeh kya hai?*'

'What did you say?'

'I said *chaku hai.*'

We laugh but not helplessly.

Then I tell her a bit, then a little more about Kulay and me but not the whole thing. She says she'll write back the next day because these days Clemmie and I can't talk much and the letters help.

I tell her how I feel like Kulay's kite hanging from a tree by a single thread, dangling and crying with vertigo.

In the early Sunday morning, the lake is bright and happy. Its waters are vast sheets of glass that gently nudge each other. In the water we can see the flowers, the white bridge and the summer house reflected upside down.

Kelsang's shed wears a huge iron lock, it being Sunday.

'What have they done to the trees?' Clemmie exclaims, pointing to the lower portions of the trees that are uniformly covered with lime to keep away the worms.

She walks angrily towards the tree that is flowering a million golden blossoms. I am about to follow her when the tramp behind the newspaper gets up and rushes towards me. I begin to run towards Clemmie who has seen him and screams, 'It's Governor, Di, it's Governor.'

I rush and grab Clemmie, feeling her heart pounding against mine and we turn towards Governor who is drunk or mad or both and stands brandishing a huge rusty knife at us.

His hair is peppered and dirty and his grotesque paunch bulges through the torn sweater.

I look down at his feet expecting to see the whitewash speckled boots that I shined long ago but his feet are bare, cracked and swollen. He stands there, neither man nor animal, frothing at the mouth and swearing at us with the words he warned us never to use when we were the wee little wondering mites and he was the man with the seven-league boots.

Clemmie has turned white. 'Let's go,' I whisper, still holding her.

A chilling breeze from the lake blows towards us. And we feel the chill in our bones as only bewildered, broken children can, children who are led into dark, drunken corners and provided for, and beaten and cruelly loved.

After the day he was seen in the lake, Governor went back to his village, staggering dangerously close to the edge of the deep gorges into which everything flowed and was forgotten. He had seen the ghosts of Damien D and Margaret M who had died in the deep ravines.

He fled to his hole in an abandoned tarred hut where he flung himself onto a pile of straw and wrapped a tattered blanket around himself though it would not stop the chattering in his head.

Finding no peace, he returned to the edge of the gorges. A leper had drawn close to him, and, touching him on the shoulder, demanded to know what caused him such anguish of spirit that he stood talking to the air.

Governor chased away the leper with his dying breath before he collapsed on the edge of the widest gorge never to rise again.

The news of Governor's death creeps through the town like the mist that entered his eyes days before he died, and turned him blind.

Reverend Ontheway decides to organise his funeral. A band of boys is sent to every house in the neighbourhood asking for contributions towards the last rites. His body is not brought to the mansion but taken directly to the cemetery, a motley kwai-eating mob following behind.

May isn't part of the crowd. Nor is she available for comment. The grapevine has it that she will soon return to the mansion whose remaining inmate continues to burden his Blue Book of Poems with anguished lines against the world.

21. MORE DEAD

Di does not dance when she learns of Governor's death. She is unable to escape the pall of gloom that has descended over the mansion and fanned out over the tenant quarters.

Ma has sought out Borthakur again and he cautions her of the great calamities that will soon submerge the mansion and its lesser parts.

'The *pagal bhoot* has gripped us all,' Borthakur murmurs, poking his teeth with a thin stick. He breaks into a loud song in praise of the Mother Goddess.

Ma watches his head shake from side to side, as he swears that it is impossible to escape from the wrath of ghosts. It seems to her that his hair, black until that moment, is slowly changing colour as he shakes it from left to right. Soon an old man takes his place.

'The worst ghosts to catch you,' the old man laughs, 'are the *pagli* ones.'

Sickened by it all, Di escapes to the lake. She does not expect to see Kulay but when she reaches the spot where they spent happier times, she almost stumbles on the boy as he lies with his face buried in the grass.

I keep my distance as I see Martin and Terri approaching Kulay. He is wearing Revise's shirt. It sits absurdly on his thin shoulders and flaps wildly as he runs away from the boys and then crashes into the grass again. He stays still on the grass. Then he pretends he is swimming. He looks ridiculous as he flaps his hands and feet on the dull grass.

Music drifts out of Kelsang's shop.

I keep my distance but when Martin and Terri move into Kelsang's shop, Kulay turns to me.

'They're coming for me in the evening.' He jumps up from the grass.

'Who?'

'Those boys.'

'To do what?'

'To fight, that's what. To fight.'

Terri reappears outside Kelsang's shop, smirking under his reversed baseball cap. He stares at Kulay as if he were a stranger.

Martin shoots out from the shop and shoving Terri out of the way, charges at Kulay and begins to kick him.

'You want to fight, huh?' Kulay punches him.

'I'll fight you tomorrow in the Bernard's playground... in front of the chicks...'

Clemmie is surprised to see Kulay in the Bernard's basketball court. They have not met since the day he turned up at May's new house with Di.

'Clemmie,' a retarded grin spreads across Kulay's face.

He begins banging the ball on the cemented ground, imitating the sing-song way in which Di announced her arrival each time she sought out Clemmie in the mansion: 'Clemmie-Clemmie I'm coming to your house...'

Clemmie is embarrassed. She wishes he would stop acting stupid and leave.

Kulay tries kicking the ball but misses. He loses his balance and falls hard on the ground. Everyone around him begins laughing. He gets up and grabbing hold of Revise, who is standing silently in the corner, drags him into the dressing room.

Clemmie winces as she hears the sound of Revise's bones being broken. She realises that Kulay is becoming dangerous. She is scared. She thinks of Di. She wonders what he has told her. She must warn her friend to be careful. She does not trust Kulay too much anymore.

Ma looks up from her knitting when I return home from the lake but says nothing. It seems I do not exist for her anymore just as nothing else exists for her except her own thoughts as she knits them into the sweater she is making. Perhaps she will weave the world into her coloured threads and everything will finally make sense in those patterns.

I walk past her and reach the end of the To-Let House. It has shrunk around me. But I am old enough to know that houses do not shrink nor do clothes grow smaller. The smuggled sunglasses of long ago are dangling from a nail in the wall. I put them on and the world turns blue. The blue postman slips a letter through a crack in the door. It is Clemmie's letter. I snatch off the glasses. It turns black and white in my hand. Ma's needles tick steadily in the background. I slip the letter into my pocket and walk boldly past Ma. She is lost in her thoughts, for even though I slam the front door, she does not call after me.

I want to get out of myself as I walk rapidly towards Kelsang's joint. But the urge passes as I step into Sunset Bar. It is beginning to fill up with people. I put my hand into my pocket and feel the fresh folds of Clemmie's letter. I can hear Kulay's voice above the din.

'So did you have a good life?' He asks no one in particular. He is sitting at the far end of the bar, almost swallowed up by the long, greasy curtain that separates the shop from Kelsang's room at the rear.

A few heads turn around but the din persists.

I squeeze into one of the benches near the front hoping Kulay has not seen me. He folds his arms and leans on the table. After a while he puts his head into his arms and begins to convulse. Perhaps he is crying. I do not go up to him. We are clearly on different sides. The crisp folds of Clemmie's letter confirm this.

I stay there until the place begins to empty out. I see Martin approaching Kulay. He catches him by the collar.

'Bloody traitor, you think you can fool the Union.'

He is dreadfully drunk and, despite my numbness, I'm scared. The lights are getting dimmer.

Martin picks up an empty beer bottle.

'I'll break this on your head.'

I'm slipping from the bench, until I'm almost under the greasy table.

Travolta emerges from behind the counter. He puts his arm around Martin and leads him to the door.

How sweet beer is when you get used to it. How light I feel. Ready for anything. The evening has given way to a cloudless night. The stars are in the lake and the wind rattles the tin roof of Sunset Bar.

By the time Di leaves Kelsang's joint, it is almost dawn. She tries to slip back into the To-Let House unnoticed, but realises that she is being watched by a shadowy figure lurking behind the curtains. Ma. As the morning light peeps through the swaying bamboo trees and lights up her ravaged face, Di fears something is amiss.

In a fit of impotent rage, Ma has gone through her things and digested a good amount of the goings-on between Kulay and Di. Above all she has read 'Wishes for My Mother,' a poem that Kulay had penned and Di had preserved in the crumbly pockets of her school coat. Ma is startled by the intensity of its hatred. The bitter woman goes on a rampage inside the meagre house and threatens to get her daughters married off to unfeeling men if they do not give in to her demands and bring under her scrutiny every shade of emotion they have ever had.

Wishes for My Mother

I wish, at this moment
You are lying on your bed

Awaiting your filthy end
And in a moment you'll be dead

I wish I could confess my sins
And make you confess yours
Get rid of the ache from beneath our skins
Before I close all my doors.

I wish I could cry then
I wish I could shed some tears
I wish it would rain then
And wash away all my fears.

I try to entrust Clemmie's letters along with my remaining secrets to Addy but Ma intercepts them.

Addy is a ferocious tiger. She claws at Ma's untouched skin and tears out the secrets from her hand. Then she crawls towards Kiyahoi's trunk but she is too big to crawl inside. So she sits at its edge trying to conceal the contents of the cardboard box that contain my secrets.

'I have spent all my money on you,' Ma screams.

Addy and I plug our ears with our fingers to stop the drone. But the cunning woman pounces on the box of letters lying in Addy's lap when she puts her fingers to her ears. Addy doubles up and does not allow Ma to get away.

Ma raves and rants and threatens to sit there without food and drink until Addy surrenders the secrets skulking in the box.

'They are no dangerous secrets,' Addy says bravely, 'But she doesn't want to share them with anyone.'

Shoving Addy to the floor, Ma pushes open the trunk and begins to drag out the things Addy had hidden there a long time ago.

Out comes the blue toy fish with a large piece of letter Addy had written to herself trailing from its mouth.

Out come the magic clothes that Addy thought grew small of their own accord.

Out comes her tiny tea-set with the little tea-pot grinning from its crack.

Out! Out! Out!

And still Addy is adamant.

And still Ma raves.

Now there is a sea of old-Addy things on the floor and Addy weeps and rubs her eyes so hard that the box slips from her wet fingers and flutters open into Ma's hands.

'Please,' I beg her but she mimics me cruelly, saying, 'I'll get you married to a man who leaves you.'

She rushes into the kitchen and brings back an old twisted frying pan. She puts Clemmie's letters into it and opening a bottle of kerosene turns it over into the pan. The letters start drowning. Their words run into the menacing liquid. Ma brings a match to the pan and they turn a fiery red in their final moments. Ma carries the blazing frying pan outside, muttering.

'You're blind Ma,' Addy cries after her.

'Don't abuse me, abuse yourself,' says Ma, shaking her greying head but the tired girls, exhausted from their outbursts, are already at the bottom of the dark blue sea.

Clemmie is frightened.

May has scarcely spoken to her since the day of Governor's death. She seems to have forgotten where she is and goes around the new house looking for things that she had left behind in the mansion.

When Clemmie finds her crouching behind a plush sofa one night, searching for the door of a tunnel rumoured to have been dug in the mansion during the First World War, she fears that her mother has lost control of her mind.

Gathering her bags, the frightened girl arrives at Benji's villa in the middle of the night.

Benji has been unable to sleep that night. The windows of the villa which rattle as gigantic trucks carrying goods thunder through the night roads, have kept him wide awake. He peeps through the glass door at the distraught girl, certain that the trucks have rattled reason out of her as well.

'So what do you think I should do?' Clemmie is flushed and wide awake.

He has allowed her to enter the villa and describe what brings her to his home at this unearthly hour. She is standing at the threshold of the door, uncertain whether to leave. She is stuck like a wrinkle on the side of his mouth and refuses to go.

Benji opens the book of sums they had been solving a few days earlier. 'Might as well get on with your maths,' he says with condescension.

She stands still. The blood rushes to her head. Her eyes glint wickedly. Her disappointed lips part in a foolish, gaping way. He grows thinner and uglier before her eyes. Thinner and uglier than the picture of him she has been drawing in her head for many days. The mental man in whom she could smuggle herself away from the world.

Mister Man, Mister Man,
Can you tell me please how the world began?

But Mister Benjamin sits unfazed as the book of half-solved sums hits his face. Then calmly putting the book aside, he rises to shut the door behind the fleeing exclamation mark.

Returning to his bed, he silently congratulates himself for having finally and fundamentally gotten over Clemmie.

On the 5th of January, 1987, Sunset Bar did not see its regulars—Martin, Terri, Revise and Kulay with or without Di.

Kelsang stands behind the counter in her den wondering why the interior does not seem quite the same. Something she has become used to isn't quite there.

At the very moment she is trying to trace the missing piece of furniture, Martin, Terri and ten other worthies are conferring in a corner of Shillong near the Government Hospital. Once they tentatively agree on the type of justice a traitor of their trust deserves, they approach Kulay, who they find sitting on the stone bench in the lake, with large, confident strides. Kulay is beaten throughout the night in a shed behind the Government Hospital.

The floor of the shed is drenched with urine and the low ceiling does not allow the five-footers to stand straight.

Neither the beaters nor the beaten are absolutely sure if the crime measures up to its chastisement.

But they beat him with heavy wooden boards, cut off his hair, burn his tongue with cigarette stubs and leave him out on the street to keep company with the stray dogs that have been unleashed by their fury at being deceived.

It is eight o' clock the next morning when the Government Hospital *chowkidar* finds the dead boy covered with a branch from the juniper pines that is sluggishly turning red.

22. MOURNING MANSION

'It was all May's fault.'

I open my eyes and hear Clemmie weeping softly beside me.

I fall to the floor. A dry, hot sob cracks my throat open.

Fear steams through the floor.

As Addy, Clemmie and I run towards the mansion, we hear someone screaming.

We bend over Kulay and beg him to wake up.

Someone standing above us says, 'dead. Spot dead.'

'It was all May's fault, anyway,' Clemmie sobs as we kneel beside twenty-year-old Kulay who is as dead as his grey, stony eyes.

'He was killed,' May yells, as she tries to force a cup of cold tea down her throat. She has returned to the mansion for the sake of the dead boy.

They have brought him back to the mansion and placed him in a highly waxed, brilliantly shining coffin.

He wears a white shirt and he is dead.

May tries to crinkle the aloneness out of her eyes. She squints slowly and blinks hard trying to get the miserable fleck of futility out of her greedy eyes.

Reverend OntheWay starts singing 'Abide with Me' in a loud tuneless voice. Despite her grief, Clemmie almost smiles. She wishes Benji were here but he has not shown up to offer his commiseration. The assembled people join in the hymn. Their voices surge through the echoing mansion as Kulay's coffin is lifted and carried out, never to return again.

Lambert Narendra Don, who, on behalf of the Union, has strongly condemned the incident, is one of the pallbearers. Wrapped in a tartan shawl, May stands at the brass-knobbed door of the mansion, watching the funeral procession inch out of the gravelled driveway and vanish through the silver wrought iron gate. A few heads appear behind her but she seems separate from the mass of mourners that has converged in the mansion.

Smoke wafts out of a black tent that has been erected at the far end of the lawn. People bustle in and out of the tent preparing a meal for the mourners. Steaming kettles of milkless tea tour the precincts of the mansion, filling clinking white china teacups.

May feels Kulay's stony eyes boring through her head. She thinks she hears the floorboards creaking under the weight of Governor's thick soled boots. Then with a start she remembers that Governor is dead, that Kulay is dead and that Redcoat has long left town. With a heavy heart, she realises that she is destined to grow old alone in the mansion. Leaving the mourners to their merriment, she disappears inside the shambles of her library and quietly shuts the door.

The sense of loss at Kulay's death occurs in slow stabbing reminders, as we sit waiting for the moon to shine the brightest than it has done in years.

That's what Clemmie's been told at school today. And yet there is nothing spectacular about the mundane moonlight flooding the room.

Addy reads out a poem she has written for her three dead kittens and for Kulay. Clemmie makes black coffee intended to keep us awake through the long exam nights. But I fall asleep dreaming of Kulay returning to the lake. His brown jacket lies near the water's edge, one arm dangling limply in the water and all the rest soft and crumpled on the paved stones.

He steps into the lake but the water turns into grass. I ask him what happened to the fish. 'The lake drowned in them,' he replies.

I wake up and am back in the dark. My mouth feels like a fish with a hook in its jaw and I am out of water and thirsty. The dark turns into Kulay's wide-open arms and they will not enfold me.

A week after Kulay's funeral, Clemmie is back at the villa. It is dark. This is the hour, rumour has it, when Father Geffen's ghost can be seen walking around the chapel beneath the ominous pines that line the driveway to Bernard's.

Clemmie has crumpled to the floor but gets up slowly. She straightens Benji's chair, picks up his books, crumples the torn bits of paper into an untidy ball and drops it in the dustbin, which is full of cigarette stubs. She has broken the window pane but she shuts the window anyway.

'Stop using my mind,' she assaults him. 'What do you want to know from me? What am I telling you that somebody else can't tell you? What am I telling you that you can't figure out for yourself?'

She can't believe she has said it but she has. She has finally cracked up.

Benji twists out a laugh. 'I'm doing nothing of the sort,' he snorts.

Clemmie stops a little bewildered. Surely he has been doing everything she accuses him of. Or has she imagined it?

'Oh...' She steps back a bit unsure.

He ignores her for sometime as she stands in the corner, trying to come to terms with the fragments of her family and friends.

Her short hair lends a startling ferocity to her elfin face, which is fevered and tired. She is crying for Kulay.

But no comfort is forthcoming from the man who has led her up the villa path and then shut the door.

'You're beautiful—too beautiful for me to mess with,' he says unconvincingly.

Is Clemmie being placated? She doesn't know. She sits on the mahogany armchair unable to move. Soon a rash grin flits across her face. The forgetful girl is beginning to remember. She sees the glint in his eyes where the love wounds have healed. She sees the road he has travelled and how he has conspired to leave her behind.

She rises in rage and with equanimity, slowly pushes him to the wall.

'Don't hit me. I'm a Christian,' he blurts out, suddenly fearful of the violence in her eyes. 'I'm a Christian,' he repeats. She bursts into a bitter laugh.

He cannot muster the courage to look her in the eye. With all the strength he can gather, he forces her to the threshold of the villa, and leaving her outside, astutely shuts the door.

Back in the mirror, I am the girl who has lost Kulay to the Snow Queen. But my face melts away the moment I turn away from the mirror. I have to stare into it again to see if I am really there.

I want to make sure that my tears are really on the verge of trickling down? I hold back the tears and begin to imagine I am in the centre of a room talking to every person I have ever known. They are all looking at me. As they look on, tears fill my eyes. My voice chokes. I cannot go on. All the people I have ever known turn around and wonder who this girl is. I have wanted so much for this to happen and it has. There I am wiping my tears and carrying on... trying to be brave... hoping they will see how astonishing I am... how truly fascinating. My clenched teeth bring me back to the cold floor. I am completely dry-eyed. Now I cannot see myself in the mirror even though I am staring hard. No one knows how long I stay there, glassy and absent.

Then again, I am speaking strange, beautiful words to them and they are completely taken in by the beauty of my voice, the passion in my face. They are mesmerised. I enthral them. They want to reach out and touch me, but I am aloof and unattainable. I stir in them a strange longing for me. Every girl wants to be like me but when they reach out to touch me I am only glass.

Though Clemmie spies the absence of love on Benji's face as he slams the door on her, she still stands there knocking until her knuckles begin to hurt.

He does not answer.

She knocks again. She will knock until her hands merge with the wood. Until wood and she are one and both can be set on fire.

They have both seen happier times. Both laughed at the Knock-Knock jokes.

'I'm a knock-knock-knocking joke. Please, please, please, please, please, please, please...' She is sobbing now.

No answer.

'...open your door.'

A woodpecker croaks in the earth's new dawn. Perhaps the sun's first rays touch him. He relents.

She has been at his door all night.

'Who's there?' his voice cranky from being suppressed so long.

'Clemmie.' Her throat full of sawdust.

'Clemmie who?'

'Clemmie-ring. You're leering at me.' She presses her face against the cold glass of the window at which he has appeared.

'Go home,' he says quietly.

'Benji, I just want to say I can't handle this anymore... I don't know what you are up to... I don't know what you want... I don't know if I'm getting it... I just know that I can't handle this anymore... so please I'm not coming any more...'

There's a big, fat bully at the door, door, door...

Clemmie's weary feet are ready to give way but she pulls them out of the ground with an immense tug of her will and begins to move away.

Benji opens his window. 'Thank God for that,' he thinks, embracing the cold cruelty that gushes into the villa through the open window. 'Got rid of her,' he says with a hypocritical smile for it is true that Clemmie has now vanished.

All he can see in the far distance is the shapely figure of Kelly the Kelsang, approaching him with self-assured strides. Perhaps Clemmie has been an apparition, he thinks flippantly. Perhaps she was a whimpering waif, he would never love again.

When the bell goes and the last paper of the exams, which will bring our school life to an end is handed in early April, 1987, I pick up my things and, feeling at a loose end, walk towards the lake. I have not been here since Kulay died three months ago.

On the grassy slopes rising up from the lake, I spy Revise with his head buried inside his sketchbook. The slopes are dotted with weekend picnickers. Some of them have spilled into the boats and are rowing energetically determined to enjoy themselves.

We gather the fallen pine needles and light a fire. Revise wanders off to get some more pine cones. I toss my empty plastic water bottle into the fire. It hisses.

Revise returns to the painting in his sketchbook. He begins to talk about strokes and lines.

'Why did they kill Kulay, Revise?'

He does not answer. My eyes travel down to the holidaymakers and I realise that they are not frolicking any longer. They have gathered around a man who is flailing his arms wildly drawing attention to something or someone inside the water.

Revise puts his sketchbook aside and runs down the slope.

I follow weakly not wanting to see who it is the boatmen are heaving out of the lake.

A man in a bright yellow turban looms above the crowd around us. He is giving instructions.

'It's the shoeshine woman.' Revise informs me with perverse persistence, even though I don't want to know who it is this time or how it happened or where it's going or what anyone can ever do.

The floating body is retrieved from the lake and covered with a plastic sheet that a picnicker quickly provides. Flies stick to the sheet. People begin to pass by the body and disperse. We pass by too.

'Kulay's main fault was that he lied.' Revise picks up his brush again. 'That's why I cannot feel sorry for him.'

'What did he lie about?'

'He said he was a blue-blooded Khasi. Only blue-bloods can join the Union.'

'He was half Khasi.'

'But he lied.'

After another long silence, I get up and go into Sunset Bar for the last time. As I enter the dimly lit back room, Clemmie pulls back the curtain and startles me. She is rummaging for Kulay's things. She pushes open the cupboard and finds his jacket among the musty hangers and boxes.

'This is a hard thing to say... but I'm leaving Shillong,' Clemmie turns her heavily swollen face away from me. 'In the meanwhile, I'm going to stay in the new house... not in the mansion.' She walks out of the shop.

The lake is empty. I keep my head down afraid to encounter the ghost of the shoeshine woman. I wonder if I should leave with Clemmie too.

Di rushes to the mansion in the hope of seeing Clemmie before she leaves. She wonders where exactly Clemmie is going. Perhaps she has a letter for her which will make everything clear.

The brass knob of the mansion door is an old bald head now, wearied by hundreds of hands that have grasped it open. No longer do the walls luxuriate in macramé, magnolia and summer sand—May's loving acrylic distempers which she once made Governor apply with punishing regularity.

Before Di can knock, May opens the door.

'Let me light the lamp before you enter,' says May, leaving Di on the doorstep outside the half-open door.

Surely the mansion has lights, Di thinks, but she is afraid to contradict the Witch.

May recedes into the dark and returns with a blackened kerosene lamp. Her fingers tremble as she brings a match close to the wick. Soon large shadows leap up onto the wall.

'Don't tell them I'm here,' she whispers.

'Who?' Di whispers back.

'I've had a gun held to my head,' she replies, peering through the half opened door to see if anyone is prowling outside.

It is late evening. The street is deserted. The men of the mansion are dead.

'Sissy Kay will become a doctor,' May informs Di in a normal voice, crossing herself at the thought that at least someone will turn out right.

She seems to have forgotten about the girl.

Perhaps she is thinking of her bottle or her Bible or of Clemmie, Di thinks wondering if she should leave.

Wild orange marigolds have replaced all the other flowers which had once bloomed in the garden. No longer the flower garden of the Witch who knew magic, Di thinks sadly, for it is true that the children have grown up and some have gone away.

'Gone far into the wide, wide world,' she expects May to say. 'I have not seen Kulay, but he will come,' she might whisper. 'Don't be unhappy, Di. Eat my fruit and admire my flowers, which are more beautiful than those in any picture book and each will tell you a story.'

Perhaps she will take Di by the hand and they will move together into the house as the old woman locks the door behind them.

But May stands motionless at the door repeating that she has had a gun held to her head, until Di is forced to leave.

It was Martin—working, when he could spare time from the Union, for a street gang. He had tied a red bandana around his head and sneaked in through the kitchen door for he knew his way about from the kite-flying-Kulay days.

Martin, the boy with a mole under his eye and a very wicked kind of nose, was now a hardened young man with a great deal of responsibility, which he discharged from time to time. Making a quiet back-door entry into the mansion, he followed the piece of piano music that was scattering itself about the house like Tom Thumb's breadcrumb trail.

May was in the midst of *Fur Elise*. Like the olden days her blouse had come unhooked and was running down her arms. She felt her step-cut hair graze her collarbones and for a moment, lost in the memories that the music evoked, forgot to breathe.

Benji, in May's memory, was caressing a drink, and had just made a brilliant remark on the piece she was playing. If she'd had an inkling of the things he was hiding from her, perhaps she might have stopped entertaining him. Having no such knowledge, she revelled in his company as her fingers flew across the piano. He had tried to keep up a steady stream of observations and she had chosen to interpret them as compliments, feeling a momentary thrill in the pleasure this self-deception evoked.

She had first played *Fur Elise* when she was barely ten after hearing Hilarious L's laborious rendition for just a week. The envious father had stooped down from the elegant piano stool to kiss the top of her head and had smelt an intuitive knowledge of music gurgling through her sunburnt hair.

'It has an air of mystery, don't you think?'

Her blouse had reached her unusually slender wrists but he was still near the curtains, a hundred steps away from her. And from that distant spot, Benji, who had been assassinated by a pair of old infant eyes, had said: 'I... won't be... coming... anymore... but... send Clemmie to me... sometimes... I'll... help her get along... Ma'am.'

The memory of that word coincided now with the opening of the heavy nut-brown door.

She looked up like a hunted squirrel and meaning to say, 'Benjamin?' said 'Martin...?' instead.

He spoke in English—reluctant and rude but lapsing into Khasi at times, especially when he mentioned the 'cause.'

'What cause?' she lashed out in English. 'Where were you when Kulay was tortured?' She was frightened but brave. The gun on her temple felt like a cold iron key. She could smell the mustard oil that Martin had used to grease it. He had bought it only the day before from a retired army colonel.

'There's money in the gun-run.' The old colonel had coughed at Martin, spewing his saliva on the young man's face. 'There's a lot of money.'

The statement had kept Martin awake at night. But now that he held the .38 to May's head he understood better what the old shit had meant.

May was quick to trace this nemesis to the scene she had witnessed in the garage many Independence Day afternoons ago but had kept quiet about. An avid believer of heaven and earth and of good and evil, she trusted, in all her earnest wickedness that the time had come to pay for her sinful silences.

Curiosity-the-cat, whose fur had turned golden with age, vindicated her sentiment by grinning from ear to ear.

This is my punishment, May thought feverishly, leading the gun-pointing lad into the kitchen. This is my punishment for keeping quiet.

The mansion was deathly quiet as it watched May at the mercy of the latest criminal the town had spawned. Ill-fed and poor once, Martin was now on his legitimate way to wealth.

Curiosity-the-cat tiptoed on her great grey paws, yawning all the while.

The large kitchen was full of smoke and Tom Dooley, as the children used to call the larder, was prematurely ajar, exuding a smell of fresh bread that crept about the house in joyous release.

May opened the door of the plum-coloured dooley and fiddled around the milk pot, bringing out the crispy cash she had stashed into its false bottom.

Martin was about to faint from the smoke, from so much money, and so much of visible womanly skin (like the olden days her blouse had come unhooked and was running down her arms).

He dug the .38 deep into her flesh and in a voice hoarse with curious longings said, 'You have more May, back in the bedroom.'

Out came the thousand five hundreds sewed into May's choicest tartan shawls—Buchanan, Gordon, Royal Stuart, Sinclair and Ogilvie. Each exotic fold was so thickly lined with dough that Martin felt he was going to cry. He saw May come towards him but she was moving so slowly, he knew she would never reach him.

He let go of his toy gun and whimpered for his own dead mother.

'My mother looked like a siren... May,' he cried, trying to grasp her in a childlike adult way.

'May, May, May,' he wept into her hair... but she let her hands remain at her sides and only said, 'My hands are tired of cooking.'

She thought she heard a blind and crippled mad man called Governor calling out her name in the echoing night streets of the town that were spawning the criminal children.

She clung to Martin fiercely.

'Do you know who killed my son?'

But Martin had recovered and disentangled himself from this mass of mother, even though her skin was fresh and incomprehensibly desirable.

He gathered the money into the shawl that Governor had chosen to wear when he felt like a piper of the Queen's own Cameron Highlanders. It was a very deep red. Just like the tapmokhlieh they had wrapped Kulay in, which was white to begin with, but slowly and surely had turned a stealthy, stunning red.

'He wasn't your son,' Martin said, and saying that stalked out of the empty house in his Leather Luv boots which were soundless and shining.

'He looked like me when they brought him,' she cried, running behind Martin as he made for the backdoor.

'Did you even see his face?' Martin snorted and turned around.

They had asked her if she wanted to see his face but she had refused. No one else had either. Of course it was Kulay.

They had dressed him in his crisp white shirt and those ridiculous drainpipe trousers. Someone had pulled up the shroud from his feet but then stopped at his chest. Who was it?

Tom Dooley was grinning a wide toothless grin and Martin had melted into the empty blackness.

> *Hang down your head, Tom Dooley*
> *Hang down your head and cry*
> *Hang down your head, Tom Dooley*
> *Poor boy you're bound to die.*

The children would dance around the plum-coloured larder with the paint splattered all over its netted door. They would sing loudly to deflect attention in case they were caught in the act of stealing something to eat.

Criminal to the core. Where were the children?

May sat herself down amidst the pumpkin leaves that had pushed their way through the door and made themselves at home all over the kitchen floor. Her knees were wobbling horribly. She put her head down on the bow-legged table with the coffee stains.

'Parents of my ardour always need the children,' she wept.

23. LETTERS 1987

May 2nd, 1987

Clemmie,

I don't know if Ma will let me go with you. I don't want to ask her. I don't want to do anything. I'm just not myself these days. I'm like a person on the way to hell. I know this doesn't make sense but when do I ever?

Clemmie, I brought in a glass wall between the world and myself, and Kulay shattered it.

He crushed it.

Do you think I'm mad? I'm having doubts these days.

Di

May 12, 1987

Di,

There is no way I can express how terribly terrible I am. I'm no longer the same either. I just don't feel the same anymore.

There is something unreal about this. Like as if it were a movie or a bad dream.

Maybe I don't want to believe it.

It's difficult to say anything because I don't know what I should or should not say.

Phoebe used to say time heals. Personally, I don't believe it.

For me, pain gets harder to bear with each passing day or at least remains as a constant reminder of the past.

But what does my pain matter? What does anything matter? Why live at all? Why? Maybe that's what Kulay thought after all.

But then I don't even know what he thought. I don't even know if I knew him.

I'm trying my best to keep feelings at zero because if I start feeling too much I'm probably going to explode against May. I cannot believe her. I'm scared I hate her as much as she once hated Kulay.

I hate her for mistreating him... I hate her men... I hate her money.

My mind seems unable to bear this hate at times and I just switch off. That's when I'm scared. I cannot remember anything about these times.

When I start plummeting like that it's very difficult to pick myself up again.

Clemmie

May 14, 1987

I'm scared I'm losing control over my mind too, Clemmie.

May 28th, 1987

Clemmie,

I've asked Ma if I can go with you a hundred times. The first few times she refused to say anything but I think she's been talking to May about it. Are you talking to May at all? If so, tell her to persuade Ma to let me go with you.

I don't think I want to stay here without you. I would have no one to turn to.

You always envied me for having a sister but Addy wraps herself inside her shell and refuses to talk. I think we've drifted too far apart now.

June 5th, 1988

Di,

I'll write clearly soon. Right now I just feel the mad urge to just do something like scream and scream sometimes and I have to bite my lips to stop myself.

June 13, 1987

Di,

May came into my room the other day as I was packing my things and started talking to me even though I kept my mouth shut.

She bragged about how she's going to pay for your studies too. I think she's told your Ma about this. Has your Ma said anything yet? It's the best thing she can do any way.

June 15th, 1987

Clemmie,

I just want to run away.

June 17th, 1987

Clemmie,

Ma came back from your house the other day and called Addy and me into the kitchen. It's the first time I've seen her in that mood—neither shouting nor silent... but still a bit sulky.

We had to sit there and listen to her going on about how my father disappeared and how she struggled and survived on her own. Then she told us she expected nothing from us either. She said she didn't care if we stayed or left.

So after some time I asked her if I can go. And she said, 'Go and stay gone.' But somehow she wasn't angry. She just seemed sad. But then that's how she's always been.

June 21st, 1987

Di,

I'm almost looking forward to a new place... new things... and people.

But there are a few things I don't know if I'll ever forget... or forgive.

I know I haven't told you much about this and I still don't want to say much. Because I can't.

It's just so hard to get myself into that state of mind when I will be able to break away from all the familiar things.

I've broken away from Benji but it's not been by choice. I had a feeling he would try to do something like this. He had tried it once before but I had won him back then.

Somehow I can't imagine not being able to run or talk to him, not expect a phone call in the evenings. It's a weird relationship, isn't it?

It will be very difficult for me to get along without him. But now I know I have to. Still, he managed to really get at me. What I had been doing to keep myself going for years fell to pieces after the day he shut his door against me.

Did I make it all up?

I know the answer to that question but it'll be easier to believe I did. It'll be easier to blame myself because at least then I can pick myself up again.

Otherwise nothing makes sense. I think I'll just crack up.

Clemmie

Still sometimes I wish he had just let me be. Anyway I'm managing fine.

So this is reality.

Where shall we go?

It might seem like a nightmare disjointed and unreal but this is the life we've got to face.

This is real.

This is true.

When we were seventeen we thought big cities were gypsies waiting to turn us inside out. Clemmie and I. We waited impatiently in peppermint airports hoping to catch planes that never looked back. We knew we must fly. Clemmie and I. May had kept her promise to support both of us and I had gratefully accepted her gift.

Clemmie and I stood in perplexing streets, praying that our paths might never stray. When cities pulled us in different directions we clung to their cloaks knowing we had a past and a place. We carried bits of our past in the dark of our pockets and waited for when the time was right to return. We were diligent and daring and studied and worked. We often slipped but never fell. We had nothing to fall back on. Still I knew that I would return to Shillong one day, if only to pay back the woman who had made our flight and freedom possible. If only to say that I still remembered Ma and May...

In my memory, it is such but we are no longer very young. Clemmie and I. We are women already as we fight back the tears threatening to spill onto Addy's letter informing us that Ma has died. We try, in our grief, to retrace the contours of her face on the last day of her life. She is late for work. She hurriedly puts on her white sari and shoving her knitting into her bag, for she always carries her knitting, rushes to catch the Iewduh-headed bus. At the fire brigade bus stop after missing a couple of crowded buses, she becomes worried at the thought of not reaching the office before the ten o' clock siren splits the air. She is conscientious and has never missed a day of work. When the next bus comes she barely manages to get a toehold on the footboard when the bus starts moving. She loses her grip and slips off the board. In a split second the rear wheels of the bus pass over her.

In our reveries it is such, and now the memory of the woman who binds Addy and me together is like a memory of something from a previous birth.

For Addy, who has never left Shillong, Ma will remain an abandoned goddess, perfumed and adorned, but contained infinitely in a halo of sadness like 'the white contains the black of the eye.'

For Clemmie, who has burnt her bridges, there is no going back and no more mourning. 'I wish I could come but it won't be easy.' She stands at the door of her studio. A strength none can shatter radiates from her serene face, no longer bitter when she says, 'somehow I feel that house never wanted me...' Then with poise she adds, 'Please be nice to May for me.'

For me, the town lies in wait, as I return to pay back the woman who had made my flight and freedom possible and wish only peace for the woman who has left me forever.

TRUCE
(1997)

24. HOMECOMING

On her journey back to Shillong, Di finds herself trying to recall more clearly what Ma had been like. But because she has evaded her for so long, memories of Ma now elude her. Still she longs for a certain clarity, though she knows that that is no longer possible. They had avoided each other from the moment it had become clear to both of them that their lives may have been set on the same path. The fear that they were destined to mirror each other had first repulsed Ma and then Di.

On the train into Guwahati, Di wonders if it had been Ma's perverse will that had tried to shape her daughter's life in the image of her own. But now that Ma was dead, she realises that she is in charge of who she is and what she is henceforth going to be. She is trying to shed the hard grip that Ma had had on her and she now believes this to be more and more possible.

A shiver runs through her as the train goes rattling across the bridge suspended high above the Brahmaputra river. Soon Guwahati will be in sight and a three hour cab ride will take her into Shillong.

The night is getting colder. The road narrower and uphill. The curves sharper. The chances of survival from head-on collisions slim. Mist rushes to meet her.

> *One misty-moisty evening*
> *When cloudy was the weather*
> *There I met an old man*
> *Dressed all in leather.*
> *He began to compliment*
> *And I began to grin*
> *How-do-you-do, and how-do-you-do*
> *And how-do-you-do again?*

The taxi driver bears her swiftly out of the railway station to a station in the Hills.

A hill station. A highland home.

Addy has moved with extraordinary energy. She has single-handedly seen to Ma's funeral, packed and moved out of the To-Let House. She has resettled herself in a second floor apartment in a busy quarter of the town. Night has fallen fast around the town as I enter it. Its sounds are muffled. A ghost town existing within the hills that, in the dark, look no longer like hills, but a shroud for the town's secrets.

Addy imparts her mild melancholy to me in a weak embrace. Her chief concern is fine discriminating thought and she has been at this task ever since I can remember. She has learnt differently from May's witchcraft. She has learnt wisely and well.

Vasalisa the Wise upto her knees in words and wisdom.

In her chiselled face, the colour of lightened wheat, I see Ma's white face even as it melts like wax under the intensity of my gaze. I hear Ma's last words, not words but silences falling into the depths of her body, turning her cold.

I am in the presence of something words cannot approximate.

Addy is patiently trying to dispose of Ma's meagre belongings. She works rhythmically placing odd things inside a cardboard box. A comb, a pair of dangling sandals, knitting needles and finally a peach-coloured wedding sari.

No longer under any obligation to rush back to Ma or escape from a censorious teacher, I luxuriate in the freedom of having nowhere to go... no people to meet. When I catch glimpses of my reflection in the shining chrome of parked cars, I no longer look for myself in them. I have found a different way of life.

Someone else, perhaps some stronger I, walks through a ragged cemetery, trying to ignore the children who hoot at me from their playing spot in the abandoned trailer of a jeep. I walk steadily until I reach the gravestone that forms my landmark.

JO WHITE

AN ARTIST

1888 - 1925

I walk around the artist's grave towards the slope at the foot of which lies:

In Loving Memory of

Kulay WILBERT

1967-1987

GOD SET HIS SEAL AND MARKED HIM FOR HIS OWN

I flop on the gravestone parallel to Kulay's. A child has followed me and tries to heave the cracking stone tip of Kulay's grave grinning at me in mischief.

'Don't...' The child embarrasses me. I don't know how to address him.

He runs off. I dig my nails into the dirty melted wax from the candles May must have lit a few weeks ago. He reappears with a bunch of flowers from a nearby shrub and sticks his hand out for some money in return. I wonder if I should accept the wild flowers. I eventually do.

The child races through the gravestones throwing up fistfuls of white sand and screaming, 'Run! Run! Run baby run.'

My unexpected meeting with May one warm June evening brings back the sharp sense of unreality I have been feeling ever since I entered the town. I have been taking a stroll down the deserted football field across which stands the mansion, wondering if the time is right to pay May a visit. The last round of tea brewing in the wooden *jadoh* stalls flavours the still air. The lights come on tentatively. In the meat shops, the flesh glows warmer under the naked light bulbs.

I must have felt her before she becomes visible to me. I turn around and find myself standing face to face with May. I watch her without wavering.

It seems as if she has never stopped crying over Kulay's death.

A bogus Baba Yaga. An old hag.

Still, it requires a strong effort of will not to turn little again in the presence of the grand old witch.

My guess is she has no idea who I am. But I am wrong.

'I saw you,' she says 'That day of the storm... I saw you with him.'

Like me, she is trapped in the past.

Two big tears spurt out of her eyes and turn them blurry. She points in the direction of the mansion. I must be crying too for the house blurs before my eyes, seeming to swirl on its chicken legs. I long to be within it with this old witch who can make magic. This is what I have been in search of. I know she can no longer hurt me. Whatever she has to say can only heal me and I find myself promising to visit her soon.

Addy comes to the steps where I am seated and puts Ma's old shawl in the sun. A sudden shower could ruin her plans. A summer storm. The few things she can't plan for in the unpredictable season.

Though I have now been with Addy a good six months, I am unable to grasp the source of the strength that has kept her going. Perhaps it is her ability to honour a diurnal routine, which is entirely of her own making. Like a nun lost in her habit, she is immersed in the thoughts that clothe her days.

From Monday to Saturday, she unfailingly trudges to the public library spending long hours in the Philosophy section. She has found her vocation in these books, even though it is hard for me to believe that she is a philosopher wanting to live alone in Shillong, imparting her knowledge to the young students of the local college she has joined.

'We have to give Ma's clothes to charity,' Addy jolts me out of my reverie.

She begins to fold the old shawl and places it neatly in the cardboard box.

Addy accompanies me on my visit to the mansion.

We put on light sweaters and scramble down the hill that leads into the main road bordering the football field. Addy leads the way. When I catch up with her, she is already at the gate, looking up at the fir pines that now keep the mansion hidden from the thoroughfare.

Our knocks remain unanswered for sometime. Just as we are about to give up, May appears on the porch behind us.

'Yes.' She squints blinking rapidly. And then the flicker of familiarity. 'Ahneee...'

She leads us into the dawn and coffee dining room. I glance at Addy, wondering if she feels an ache too. She is staring at the mantelpiece from which five-year-old Clemmie bursts out of a dusty photo frame.

'I'm an old timer now,' May's eyes are shadowed by dreams of the dead. 'I'm an old timer but they still won't leave me.'

We keep silent expecting her to say more.

'I told you the bad fairies appear at one o'clock,' she says suddenly, referring to the hour Kulay died.

She refuses my offer to pay her back the money she gave me, finding it difficult to focus on the present moment.

Addy glances at her watch but the mansion seems to chide her for keeping time.

I look at May as she sits staring at the mantelpiece. Her mouth is slightly parted, as if she were gasping at Governor. But no men share her solitude.

'I miss your Ma,' she says, seeming to remember that she has something more to tell us.

'She suffered... struggled so much... died so sadly.'

Addy and I silently weep with her words.

25. ADIEU

'Unless I'm hounded out of Shillong, I won't leave it,' Addy says in response to my decision to leave a few days later. She is in the midst of a piece of knitting when I tell her I have decided to go.

My imminent leave-taking heightens my perception of everything around me—the way the light falls, the slow coming to life of the shops, the bird songs, even the crackers which one could mistake for gunshots.

She pushes her unruly hair that slips out of its clasp and troubles her eyes.

'Sister Christine has cancer. I'm knitting her a muffler.' She has developed a fondness for the old convent school ever since the day she returned there to give Ma's belongings to the nuns who would pass them on for charity.

Addy measures the muffler. It starts at her foot and reaches all the way round to the other foot via the back of her neck.

Perhaps her ability to get absorbed in things will make my departure less burdensome.

She neatly puts her knitting aside and creeps back into her book as if to say, 'I am a loner. I thrive in solitude.'

The mild flavour of sadness that accompanies the end of something creeps through the house.

In the evening, I walk into town. I am arrested by my memories of the past and hear the immutable sound of my love for the town, for May, Ma, Addy, Kulay and Clemmie ringing in the quiet streets and in the fields where the schoolboys gather to play cricket in the evenings. It is a sound that is slowly dissolving the bitterness in me. I realise that it is love that has finally saved me. I understand, then, that there can be no escape from this deafening love. It is final.

I read Clemmie's week-old letter again. She is convinced that she is destined to revisit the mansion only when May is dead. She will inhabit the house she was born in, open out the windows and bring back the flowers. But she must wait for May to go.

Meanwhile, she awaits my return.

As I prepare to leave, Addy moves around our almost empty house cautiously, not wanting to disturb the unearthly silence that has crept in and is settling down. She is lost in herself unable to understand time's terrible incoherence.

Soon I shall tear through this web of memory and never return. When I am gone the town will curl up into mist and blow back into the chimney of the little clay hut inside the book that is lying in the depths of the iron trunk that has sunk to the bottom of the dark blue sea.

I get onto the Long Round Road, past the lake to which I shall never return, past Little Rose Convent, past the Gurudwara, past all the familiar child-scapes which bring back memories on waves of colour and detail.

On the way, it begins to rain. I try to cut through the water but the rain is intense.

I enter a stationary bus, pulled up by the side of the road, and roll up the windows.

The glass gets steamy.

The driver takes out a rag and wipes the windshield.

Everything turns silent. The vast blue hills in the distance envelop the rainy town. The rain shatters the roof of the bus and then the hailstones come. I begin to wipe the glass with my hand. The dripping trees come into view. Their brown pine needles are soggy. The tiny white crystals hit the glass and happily dart to the road. The ash from the forest fires has turned white and the trees on the slopes look like they are flowing. But it is only the rain on the glass turning things fluid.

A fever burns my eyes. My hot hand sizzles on the cold window of the bus. There is grey water as far as I can see. A truck goes by loaded with wood gone weak with water. The men on top of the truck shout out to us. The bus driver hits his horn in response.

We stay there silently for a long time.

A woman and a girl huddled under a yellow shawl climb up the hill in the distance and disappear.

I want to disappear too and I want to disappear without bitterness.

Borthakur is standing at the door of his quarters, squinting at the mist rising above the mansion's roof, when I visit the place for the last time. I have entered from the back avoiding the front gate and the chance of bumping into May.

He hasn't recognised me.

When he meets my eye, I try to pretend I have come to meet May.

He shakes his head.

I fear she is dead.

'Disappeared.'

Through the remaining days of my stay, it will come to light that May has last been seen on a bus bound for the village of Myl. Some will swear that she has flung herself from the highest gorges crying out like the mythical Likai, who has drowned herself in the waters for having unknowingly eaten her child's flesh.

For the moment, however, I stand beside Borthakur in comforting anonymity.

The mansion is obscured by the mist. The fir pines hem in its secrets which are alive only within me. They are redeemed in the remembering like Borthakur's freshly washed sheets.

And I bear neither any malice.

Acknowledgements

This book would not have existed without the people behind Tara Books – V.Geetha, Gita Wolf and Sirish Rao. To them I am hugely indebted for believing in my writing, painstakingly honing it and presenting it to a wider audience. Their commitment to meaningful literature is exemplary and it has been a privilege to work with them.

Deep gratitude to my father, Noorul Hasan, for his editorial comments on several versions of the novel, to my mother, Santosh Hasan, for her enthusiastic reception of the novel and to Nafis Hasan, for his steady support both from within and outside Tara.

To Philip Bounds, deep gratitude for his steady inspiration and sharp humour.

To Anjum Hasan, and Zac O' Yeah, I am indebted for literary advice and encouragement at every stage of this novel.

Adil, Zarin and Bulbul– thanks so much for your feedback and warnings!

'Uncle' Vincent, Nigel Jenkins, Sanjib Kakoty, Masood Khan and Mark Swer have also inspired me either by their own work or by their conversations with me.

Finally to those who have been important to this novel but wish to remain anonymous I give my heartfelt thanks.